When a Dream becomes a Nightmare

David I Brown

Sorrell Books

Acknowledgements

THIS IS A STORY about Peter Ianson, the painter in "Painting the Taj Mahal". It is a sequel, of sorts, and covers his relationships with people he meets as he lives and paints in Berwick upon Tweed, for an exhibition in the summer. However, terrible things start to occur that ruin many lives and relationships.

I am grateful to all the brilliant internationally known writers, whose works have inspired and helped me express my thoughts in telling this story. Also big thank you to Phil for proofreading.

also by David I Brown

Cancer Was My Companion: A Memoir
Jab Jab Molassi at the Break Point Hotel (Illustrated)
Break Point Hotel (Revised)
Painting the Taj Mahal
Secrets of Istanbul

Chapter 1

The dark grey skies over the English Channel are never the easiest to paint with passion and depth. They tend to be monotone and, well, just boring, so I thought, as I sat in the shelter of an old wooden fishing boat on the shingle beaches of East Preston in West Sussex.

I used to live further along the coast, at Elmer Sands on the other side of Littlehampton, but with several big commissions and some successful exhibitions, I had been making good money over the past few years, and was able to afford somewhere, well, more upmarket. My father had always said that I was never good enough to be a painter of distinction, and he believed that even good painters were always financially poor - until they died, of course.

East Preston had some large expensive properties, not that I owned one, but it meant that the coffee shops were always full and costly, the restaurants busy and the two pubs raucous with those that had plenty of money, on a Saturday night. Still, I liked the village, and my rambling brick and flint cottage facing the sea, even with all that the weather threw at it, it was always warm and cosy.

The early Spring weather was still cold, sharp and miserably wet. The South westerly winds could be bitter and I found my numb fingers were barely gripping the pencil they had between them. It was early March and I was still alone, as indeed I had been for the past few years since the love of my life, had left me for a much better man. That was at the same time that I went to India to paint a commission, and what I thought was going to be a very lucrative family portrait in front of the Taj Mahal in Agra. It had become a shocking and upsetting time in my life with the murder of my patron's wife and almost a similar fate for that of his two young boys. I had often thought of them as I did again now, sitting on my little canvas folding painter's seat, with a pad of sketching paper in my lap and a well used HB pencil stuck between my lips. Being chewed. They would be in their late teenage years now, I mused, as the sun broke through the mud grey clouds, just for a second or two.

I looked up to catch it disappearing again as the black clouds and darkening sky raced over me and deposited large droplets of icy rain water on my head and sketch pad. It was time to go. The cottage wasn't far away and in my mind, I could hear the kettle boiling and smell the tea already brewing, as I struggled with my little seat and backpack, walking almost doubled up, with the full force of the wind and now cold sleet, in my face. By the time I reached my front door, the chilling wetness was already seeping through all the layers of clothing I had on. A little cold rivulet of water had found its way inside my jacket collar and was now trickling down my neck. With soaked trousers and squelchy shoes, I was exceptionally pleased to get the front door open, tossing the backpack and seat inside and allowing the wind to slam the door closed violently. I stood for a second or two cursing the weather and feeling very cold, wet and miserable. Such was my life. I had a hot shower and was trying to keep the sketches I had drawn, flat enough under a towel to try and dry them out. It wasn't working and the crinkled paper and smudged lines just disappointed me still further as I sat down slowly to finish the remains of a cup of strong Yorkshire tea.

I sat there drying my hair with my towel when I noticed an envelope on the table. It was addressed to me, of course, but I hadn't opened it earlier as I had picked it up off the doormat and dropped it on the kitchen table as I left that morning. It was also crinkled, as wrinkled as my sketch pad papers and I had difficulty in opening it without it tearing. Inside was quite a surprise. To my astonishment, it was an invitation to go and paint alongside a well known Scottish artist, George Bellingham, on the banks of the River Tweed, in Northumberland. I smiled at the thought and quickly agreed in my mind that I would go. He was offering me a little cottage to rent on the South side of the river near Berwick, and the tuition would be free, provided I agreed to exhibit my work along with his in June.

Remembering an old geography book I had about the Cheviot Hills and the Border Country. I found myself rummaging around the bookshelves in the study trying to locate it. Finally, I espied it on the top shelf. It smelt a little musty and the cover had faded quite a bit. Running my finger down the index, I found the chapter on "The River Tweed". Settling down on the sofa, listening to the rain hammering against the window panes, I eagerly read through the short chapter. I realised it was quite a long river stretching from high in the Lowther Hills to the West then flowing some ninety-seven miles across the scenic border region in Scotland and northern England. The Scottish Gaelic name is Abhainn Thuaidh. I couldn't even pronounce it correctly let alone remember it. The one thing I did remember, was that Tweed cloth derived its name from a strong association with the river. The name "Tweed" could be an Old Brittonic name, it said, meaning "border" and its destination is the breakwater at Berwick Upon Tweed, which is where I was going to be heading for. Amazingly it is the fourth longest river in Scotland, my book continued to tell me, and it takes great pride in the fact that it produces more fish caught to the fly than any other river in Britain. As it's so clean, it's home to a range of wildlife, but especially salmon, which draws anglers to its banks from all over the country. I think I read somewhere too that Peebles, which is further up the river from Berwick, has its Latin motto associated with the river. "Contra Nando Incrementum" which means to flourish by going against the flow. Seemingly, it draws painters to it as well, I pondered, which also seemed to go against the flow of fishermen and wildlife.

The Chapter wasn't a very long one and therefore failed to provide much more information, but there were some beautiful, if old, photographs of various places and bridges. I especially liked the ones of the Royal Border and Coldstream Bridges and made a mental note to ask George if we would be painting either or even both of them. Putting my feet up on the sofa, I closed the book and rested it on my chest, closed my eyes wondering what might be in store for me up on Northumberland's cold and windy coast, painting and living at the mouth of such a beautiful river.

Chapter 2

A couple of weeks later, I was heading North. I had decided to visit friends in London which let me take the longer but easier route up, via the A1. My transport was a newish Land Rover. I had another car, a renovated Triumph Herald Vitesse soft top. Its sills and doors used to have more filler in them than metal, and the rebored six cylinder engine leaked more oil than it used. After some new body parts, a new engine and a total makeover, it made it a great old vintage for tootling around Sussex, but I thought my trusted and rugged Land Rover might be better for a river painting expedition up in the Border country. It made for an arduously slow and rather hard ride along the A1, requiring more fuel stops than I had initially anticipated.

Pulling in for, yet another diesel, tea and pee stop at a petrol station just outside Wetherby in Yorkshire, I parked close to the kiosk, general shop and burger bar and rushed in to find the toilets, before grabbing a mug of hot tea and a newspaper.

Although it was early Springtime, the weather was kind and the mid afternoon sun's rays were quite uplifting and warm. As I had my head buried in the sports pages, I hadn't noticed the two guys walking towards me across the carpark.

"Err, excuse me!"

Although the sun was in my eyes I saw the outlines of two young men about my age I thought. As they drew closer and stood over me, I could see that one was Indian with a curly mop of hair and a huge coat hanger smile, the other was taller, with wire rimmed glasses and wearing a big thin lipped grin.

"We were just wondering if you had a car? We are heading North and thought you might give us a lift."

The Indian guy had a neatly trimmed beard and a row of white teeth that sparkled in the sunlight that matched the twinkle in his eyes.

"I do, but there isn't a lot of room if you've got a load of luggage." I said, looking from one to the other as they stood holding a rucksack each. They presented their only belongings, the two oversized rucksacks, and looked at me with more than a hint of hope on their tired faces.

"Where are you heading to?" I asked with a little sigh.

"I'm heading to Berwick, Berwick upon Tweed. Would that help?"

"Wow, that's where we are heading too, what a coincidence." Replied the guy with glasses. His accent suggested he was Canadian or American. I never was very good with accents. I guessed that that had no idea where Berwick was, let alone it being their destination, but what the heck. I could do with the company I thought and they didn't look like muggers or worse, murderers.

"Okay, come on then." I said happily, pointing to my Land Rover and folding up my newspaper.

"Oh my," croaked the guy with the accent, "A real British Jeep. Looks as tough as an old tank." He said and chuckled.

"Hey! Less of the *old* my friend." I interjected, "It's only a few years old and it's giving you a lift."

He chuckled again.

"Hey, excuse me, no offence intended. Always wanted to ride one of these. It's going to be great."

I opened the rear door, holding my stuff back to prevent it falling out as they tossed their two huge bags on top of mine. The door had to be closed quickly to prevent everything tumbling to the ground, as we all climbed in.

They offered me some cash for fuel, but I said it wasn't necessary, but they could stand me a beer when we reached Berwick.

Land Rovers are not renowned for being fast nor particularly quiet, so it was going to be an interesting but hopefully, a fun journey.

Having filled up we set off to continue our journey. I was quite thankful for the company really, and it wasn't long before we were exchanging names and some personal details.

The North American accent sat in the front alongside me and he introduced himself.

"My name's Rick. Well, Richard actually, but don't call me Dick," he said with a warm chuckle, "and this is Jaspal." Indicating repeatedly to the back seat, with his thumb.

"I'm a Sikh from the Punjab originally, well not practising, but it means a venerable man or a great man, if like my dad you are over 50."

He laughed and I caught his wonderful smile and a row of white shining teeth, in my mirror.

"I am called Jaspal Singh. Singh is my surname and it means *lion*, but most people think I'm just a pussy cat really. It is the name given when you are baptised and a fairly common name in Sikh communities. You can call me Jas, everyone else does."

"So it's Rick and Jas then?" I said with a hesitantly pathetic laugh.

"Sounds like you should be on TV in a comedy show, like Eric and Ernie in *Morecambe and Wise*."

Neither of them laughed. Perhaps the trip wasn't going to be that much fun after all.

"I'm Peter." I said trying to lighten things up again. "You can call me whatever you like, but most people stick with Peter."

"Well, okay," Rick said slowly, "but I guess I'll call you Pete, just to keep everything - simple."

"Where are you from Rick? The accent sounds American, but perhaps that's an insult, if you are from north of the border." I said hedging my bets.

"Hey good job you said that, cause I'm Canadian," he chuckled again and smiled a wide thin lipped smile. "Brought up in Montreal, but I was actually born here in England and not far from where we are going, in a place called Middlesboro."

His pronunciation of Middlesborough would have perhaps created some mirth with the locals.

"Berwick is a little further north than that, but I suppose you'll be in the general area. Going back to your roots are you?" I muted, glancing sideways at him to see his reaction.

"Yeah, I guess so. My father was an engineer there, in the fifties, but we had to move to Canada when I was small. I have a cousin up there though."

There was a sudden silence when he turned to look out of the window, as if to hide a secret, or something painful that had caused them to suddenly leave the city. I glanced in the rear view mirror.

"Why are you going to Berwick Jas?" I said, leaving Rick with his thoughts.

"No job. Running away." Jas said and sighed quietly.

Rick clicked back into the conversation.

"Running away from his girlfriend in London, he means." Said Rick with a smirk, turning round to look at Jas and raising an eyebrow, creating a set of deep wrinkles across his forehead.

"We both finished our Chemistry Degrees last summer and have been living in a house on Clapham Common, with three nurses and an old Sicilian couple who were dealing in their Embassy's *excess* alcohol supplies. I've got a couple of bottles of their *fig and orange liqueur* in my rucksack." He screamed gleefully.

"Nobody else could stand it, including me. Thought I would sell it to some poor unsuspecting person in Berwick."

We all laughed and settled back as the heavy traffic suddenly slowed us down to a crawl. It was going to be nightfall before we reached the Border Country.

Chapter 3

It was late afternoon by the time we had reached the outskirts of the town. It had dawned on me that my two new companions probably hadn't anywhere to stay, but as I had the keys to my accommodation, even though I didn't know what it was really like, I knew it had three bedrooms and it was just as easy to invite them to stay the night, at least.

It was cold and the wind off the sea was quite vicious as we drove over the narrow Royal Tweed Bridge and turned right, into MaryGate. It was grey and the blackened buildings from decades of smoke from coal fires weren't particularly welcoming.

I pulled into a space in front of some forlorn looking shops outside the North Hotel off to the right, and rummaging around in the glove compartment, found the scrap of paper that I had scribbled the address on.

Crab Cottage
Main Street
Spittal

Where the hell is this place called *Spittal,* I thought, reading it again.

A small framed woman in a dark maroon coat was struggling up the street. She was almost bent double, fighting against the wind. The arch through the walls, at the bottom of the street, framed her nicely.

As I pulled on the handle of the Land Rover door, the wind caught it and wrenched it open. The blast of cold air rushed into the cabin, and caused my passengers to hurl a tirade of abuse my way. Ignoring them, I grabbed my jacket, struggling to get it on with the gale blowing.

"Excuse me," I shouted, nearly losing the piece of paper as I tried to hold my jacket closed.

"Can you tell me where Spittal is?"

"Aye laddie. It'll be back over the wee bridge. On the other side of the river." She mouthed against the wind, trying to steady herself.

I caught her arm when the wind caught her as she tried to stand more erect and steady herself. Nearly dropping her heavy shopping bag, while trying to keep her hat on, she nodded towards the river and the bridge that we had just crossed.

Driving back over the bridge, we saw the sign for Spittal and the Dock Road. It looked grim and I could tell from the silence that the other two weren't very impressed either. As I swung the Land Rover around an 'S' bend, a huge wave had hit the harbour wall and without warning, had landed right on top of the jeep. What started as a wall of white, suddenly turned dark for a second or two. We all felt the Land Rover move sideways and once the wave had subsided, salt water running off the windscreen, we were all horrified to find that the wave had moved us to within a foot of the edge.

"Bloody hell!" I muttered, my heart racing.

"Gee. Wow. Amazing!" Was all that Rick could muster with a huge coat hanger smile on his face. His eyes were out on stalks and looked huge. His glasses had been knocked off and lay at his feet.

Jas just sat motionless on the backseat with both arms outstretched, as if he were frozen in time.

The rest of the drive along the main street was taken at a much slower pace, as I felt my heart beat slow, despite having to listen to the manic chatter from the other two.

At the far end, we finally found "Crab Cottage". It was a single storey, grey rendered building and bigger than I expected. It was at the end of a row of similar cottages and surprisingly long. The road stopped just beyond it, where the yellow sandy beach started. Above the beach, the low cliffs rose up to what looked like a small tower.

The wind was blowing sand up the street. It was then that it dawned on me, why no one else had ever wanted to live there and why it was a peppercorn rent.

"Well, here we are. Home sweet home." I said trying to smile, as I gritted my teeth both with the cold and the sheer disappointment of my new *accommodation*.

The other two started to unload the Land Rover, while I charged down the old oak door with my shoulder after unlocking the door with a rather large and rusty key. The mountainous pile of pamphlets, letters and fliers provide to be quite a challenge in gaining entry.

It was dark and smelt of seaweed and mould. The curtains were closed which made for a rather grim entrance. Still the lights worked, as we found out when Jas flicked on the hall switch and a dim bulb at the far end lit the sad grey white space.

A rug covered the stone tiled floor, but its bare pattern was little comfort. Two bedrooms led off the hall to the right and to the left, with a third at the end. There was a small but cosy lounge diner. In it was a breakfast bar with shelves above, that divided the space. There was no central heating but at least the wood burner looked as if it had been well used and would still be functional. Several logs, covered in spider's webs, sat awkwardly in a wicker basket next to it. We all sighed when we opened the bathroom door. The big iron bath had rust stains streaking down it from the dripping taps. A black crack in the sink looked even more depressing and none of us dared raise the lid of the toilet.

I switched on the water heater with a little trepidation. The red glow from the bulb, at least gave us hope that it might be functioning, just.

The view from the back of the cottage was amazing though. We all stood and gazed at the stormy sea and crashing waves that pounded the pale sandy beach just beyond the old picket fence. There was a gate that was hanging by one hinge. It didn't move as it was well cemented in a deep drift of sand. All that there was of the garden were a few green pendants of grass that stuck out of the ever shifting sand, as the wind blew it horizontally, making it into little dunes.

"Awesome." Rick chuckled. It was a statement that I knew was going to be repeated regularly and would end up becoming a little bit annoying.

A couple of hours later, with the contents of the Land Rover deposited on the lounge floor and a roaring fire going in the wood burner, we all sat as close as possible to it, each with a bottle of Newcastle Brown Ale in one hand and a Northumberland sausage roll in the other.

Rick had braved the windy weather and walked up to the local grocers shop and bought whatever had been available. Beer seemed to have been more on his mind than milk, although he did buy our dinner. To him, it seemed quite reasonable that dinner would mean a whole packet of dried spaghetti to cook, to which he would add a whole half pound of cheese and a complete bottle of tomato ketchup.

Jas and I were past caring as we opened our second bottle of beer and I put another log into the wood burner, before sitting back into the dark blue velvet sofa. It had seen better days and smelt like the rest of the cottage, but I didn't care as my eyes closed a little.

My new adventure had started. I had finally arrived in Berwick, was looking forward to meeting up with George to paint and I had acquired two new friends on the way.

The following morning, I woke early. I had not slept well. The windows rattled until the wind had eased, and the mattress was damp and uncomfortable. I had somehow made the bed, whilst the other two had slept in their sleeping bags in the next room. There were two old single metal framed beds in the other two bedrooms, so I had left them to sort it out themselves as I closed my door, and still fully clothed, eased my tired body under the damp duvet.

Pulling back the old heavy curtains, the light reflecting off a choppy North Sea, was electric. The morning sun in a pale blue sky with racing clouds, immediately lifted my spirit as I stood amazed at the vista of frothy waves and flat wet sands. Although it was still early, I did have things to do besides admire my new view. I was due to meet George in some cafe on MaryGate, opposite the junction to a road called Eastern Lane. We had driven down MaryGate the night before, so I knew it probably wasn't too hard to find. I put the kettle on as I got my painting bag together. Having not undressed the night before, a shower and some fresh clothes were needed. It wasn't until I checked in the bathroom and realised that the *shower* I was expecting to find was an old hand held plastic one, with a shower head and hose with two rubber connections to the hot and cold taps in the bath. I closed my eyes and cursed, switching on the boiler in the hope of creating enough hot water.

The kettle had boiled but as we hadn't any milk, I took a cracked mug of instant coffee back to the bathroom and ran the water. Surprisingly, the boiler hadn't blown up and even better was producing hot water. The fact that it was the colour of Burnt Sienna, was another matter.

Having shaved, suffered an orange shower, and dressed in whatever came out of my suitcase first, I was ready to leave, when Jas opened the bedroom door. His hair was a black mass of gentle curly waves and his smile a row of gleaming white teeth shining through his well trimmed beard.

I could see that Rick was still asleep, curled up in his sleeping bag in the darkened room.

Jas was naked except for a pair of baggy pants and he wrapped his arms around himself complaining how cold it was.

"I'm on my way out, Jas, but the water in the kettle is still hot. No milk I'm afraid and only coffee, no tea." I said, as I gathered up my jacket and bag and headed down the hall. "Help yourself." I shouted as I closed the front door and headed off.

Chapter 4

The cafe was empty when I arrived, except for a couple of workmen having a full on cooked breakfast including a couple of slices of fried haggis on the side. Up the top end of the street was the stone arched gateway and stalls were being prepared. It was obviously market day.

My coffee was fresh and welcoming and as I stared at the workmen with their full on breakfasts, I suddenly realised just how hungry I was.

I was just ordering toast and scrambled eggs when George arrived, rubbing his hands together.

George was quite a thoughtful Scottish gentleman. He was probably twice my age with short salt and pepper hair and wore a very trendy pair of blue framed glasses. Although he was quite shy I thought, he had a wicked twinkle in his eye and I just knew we would get on very well together."Peter?" He enquired immediately, thrusting out his right hand in greeting.

"Sorry about the cold hand. Late March in the Borders is still a wee bit colder than your South coast is, at this time of year," he apologised. "I'm a wee bit late too. This time in the morning is a little early for me."

"I've just arrived myself, George. Do you mind if I call you George?" I said realising that I had been a little presumptuous.

"Not at all, Peter. We are two artists together. Kindred spirits and all that. First names are a *must* in my book." He smiled and grasped my arm.

"I see you've already ordered your breakfast."

"I am sorry. Would you like some too?" I said, feeling a little embarrassed for not waiting.

"Aye, I will do that, Peter. Whatever you are having, I'll be having the same. Very kind of you to offer." He said with a grin as he walked over and sat down by the window.

I hadn't realised that I would be paying for his breakfast as well, and wondered if this was going to be expected, whenever we ate out together.

He suggested that we take a drive up to a couple of places along the northern side of the river bank, a few miles inland, as he thought they gave excellent vistas for us to paint, although he was a little concerned that his car might get stuck in the mud in places.

"Oh, that won't be a problem. I have a Land Rover, which will easily cope with a few soggy fields and muddy ruts." I enthused and then suddenly realising, as a big smile grew across George's face, that I had set myself up again.

On the way into town, I had stopped at the 'S' bend and looked through the window at the three bridges that crossed the Tweed, almost at the same point where we were nearly washed away the night before, with the old Royal Bridge in the foreground and behind it the newer main road bridge A little beyond that, was the majestic rail bridge, "The Royal Border Bridge", to give it's proper name. The huge viaduct that spanned a wide curve in the river. I knew I had to paint that view of the bridge and the way the river curved beyond it. The early morning spring sunlight was glorious, as it shone on them all and made them glow.

I drove over the old bridge and down towards Turret Walk where I noticed an Art School in the far corner by the town walls. There, I saw another, but different view of the same three bridges, this time with Tweedmouth, nestling in between them.

An hour later we were struggling to get some traction across a meadow having found a track and managed to get through an old wooden gate and into a field that led down to the river. I stopped, just before the bank dropped away and was awestruck at the beauty of what I saw. The gentle curve of the wide river, and trees on either side with just the hint of fresh spring green as the budding leaves were just beginning to open. The sun shone on the water from the South now, and the reflecting light took my breath away. The tide was dragging the dark waters quickly towards the mouth of the river at Berwick, by the coast and then out to sea. Occasional and suddenly, a series of concentric circles would appear on the surface that would widen as they raced away with the current. A heron stood perfectly still, as if a statue, on a lower branch of a magnificent beech tree whose boughs almost touched the water.

George saw the look on my face as I limply waved an arm in the direction of the river, wide eyed and grinning like a demented Cheshire cat.

"That will be the salmon, Peter," George said, knowingly. "I guess you are well informed about how superb the River Tweed is for its salmon fishing."

"Indeed, I do." I replied, faintly as the words got lost in the sounds of the river.

"I'll take you to the 'Smoking Huts' in Eyemouth, next week, and you can see the traditional ways of smoking the fillets, still used today. Maybe we can do some painting and buy a wee fish or two as well. The Bell Tower at the golf course is another place for a good study, too."

The smile on his face and the glint in his eye reminded me of the same look he gave me as I paid for his breakfast in the cafe earlier.

Still, It was truly a wonderful place to paint.

I was eager to do some sketching and so we both gathered our pads, pencils and mini camping stools to sit on, from the back of the Land Rover, and found a place in the sun, down the sandy bank and away from the cold wind that still blew from the North, as it had done since I had arrived. It was a glorious time.

I felt alive, and with such a well respected artist at my side, and the thrill of producing some excellent water colours with the guidance and help of my new tutor, I thoroughly enjoyed the morning.

A flask of black tea was all we had for lunch. I had forgotten to bring anything, and George, quite obviously, wasn't one for taking a break for lunch and hadn't brought anything else but his small thermos flask.

It was getting chilly and we decided to call it a day, mid afternoon. I dropped him off in the centre of Berwick, having agreed to meet the following morning, a little later than today, so that I could drive us to Coldstream, to sketch the bridge there after having breakfast at the cafe again.

I had just parked the Land Rover outside the cottage and was standing with my hands on my hips, looking at the mud caked wheels and bodywork, when Rick opened the front door and stared at it as well.

29

"Awesome! Amazing!" He said, grinning.

"You had a good day?"

"Yep, thanks Rick. George took me to a great location a couple of miles up river, to do some sketching and painting. It was truly *awesome*!" I said smiling, as I teased out the last word.

"Come on in," he said. "Jas is cooking curry."

I had the distinct feeling that the two of them had already settled in quite nicely, and were perhaps going to be staying for more than a couple of days.

Although I was a little annoyed at being taken for granted, the idea of having some company was actually rather comforting, and they did seem to be nice guys.

Rick handed me a Cobra beer, as I just dumped all my painting gear and the bag, in my room. The exotic smells of coriander and garlic, ginger and cardamom made my nostrils flair and my stomach ache. I was hungry and couldn't wait.

Jas was busy in the kitchenette, with pans all over the place and vegetables in the sink, and chicken pieces ready for chopping.

He had some rock music on. I would come to learn a lot about Jas and his choices in music!

"Hey man, just chill out while I prepare dinner. Go see the sea or something. This is going to be amazingly awesome."

I nearly said something in reply but decided against it and headed towards the patio doors that opened onto the sandy garden and the beach beyond.

"Rick said, he really likes my hot curries, so he is going to get one." He shouted after me, even though most of it was drowned out by the music behind me and the sound of the pounding waves in front of me, so it didn't really dawn on me what he had actually said.

An hour later I understood - totally.

Rick's challenge to Jas, to make the hottest curry he possibly could, was an obscene understatement.

Although there were three of us having dinner sitting round the small table, only one was quite happily eating his fill. The other two, namely Rick and I were already on our fourth pint of water and our second toilet roll. The toilet rolls had been necessary, in order to mop up the continuing torrents of sweat that poured easily from every pore of our sweat soaked brows.

Rick had taken off his glasses, as they were too steamed up and uncomfortable to wear, and he no longer had his silly grin on his face, and he never mentioned the word awesome, once, not once, ever again!

We had soon had enough, and Rick and I needed to get some fresh air.

He and I spent the next several minutes enjoying, for the first time, the freezing cold wind as we marched headlong to the dashing waves on the shore line. The tide was in and the sound of crashing waves was spectacular.

We smelt the sea and breathed in the ozone, albeit through curried nostrils, and managed a glass of malt whisky each as we stood in the dark, within an inch of the tide line and felt the wind stream through our hair, ridding us of the smell of curry as well as cooling us down.

Jas, was tasked with washing up, as penance, but as we saw him dancing wildly to his rock music in the lounge, I guessed he was more than happy with that. After all, he had won the challenge.

Rick, on the other hand, wasn't at all happy and whilst he pretended that it was all just good fun, I could see in the narrowing of his eyes and the tightening of his jaw as he joked about the experience, that underneath it all, he was quite upset.

The guys had bought a TV for us to watch. It was a thank you present for allowing them to stay.

"Thank you so much for the TV, by the way," I said, a little suspiciously. "That's rather generous of you," I continued. "How long did you say you were intending to hang around?" I mused, with a raised eyebrow whilst folding my arms in a mocking inquisitor's stance.

"Hey, man. We can pay some rent and help with the food and electric bills. Well, for a few weeks anyway." Rick said, shuffling his feet and looking over his glasses at me with his usual silly grin.

"And I'll do the cooking." Jas said eagerly.

With that remark, both Rick and I hurled the sofa cushions and abuse in equal measure, at him.

The following morning the wind had completely dropped, the sea was calm and I was looking forward to spending more time sketching and painting with George again. It was Friday, so the upcoming weekend would allow me to explore Berwick and sort out the cottage, buy food and talk more with my new found tenants, about how we were going to make living together work well.

I couldn't find a space to park outside the cafe, so drove around until I found a carpark under the defensive walls that surrounded part of the old town. Solid, imposing and blackened stone work. Before that, I had gotten lost and found myself outside the old Infirmary, with a statue of a lady I didn't recognise. George was already sitting by the window with a coffee, by the time I got there. He was waiting for me to arrive before he ordered breakfast.

"Full breakfast again, Peter." He said as I lent over him, hands on the table.

It was less of an enquiry and more of a command. I dutifully, but slowly stood upright and strolled to the counter, and sighed, before looking back at George's glowing face.

A couple of hours later, we arrived at Coldstream Bridge. George instructed me to pull over into a lay-by just before the bridge. We parked up and got out into the delightful spring sunshine and scrambled down the bank of the river to seek out the view of the bridge.

"This is fantastic, George," I announced gleefully. "Can we just go and have a look at the bridge for a while? I understand it represents the border between England and Scotland."

We walked along the road towards the bridge, whilst George explained that it had been designed by John Smeaton, and had been started in 1763 and finally completed three years later. It was a beautiful bridge and majestically spanned the Tweed as well as the border. Originally being a Toll Bridge, it was a few hundred metres

33

below Coldstream. On the other side of the bridge, the town of Cornhill, sat neatly in the woods.

"So, there are seven arches George," I said, pointing them out. "Although, the two smaller ones at either side, the flood relief holes, are blocked with branches and rubbish."

The reflection of the arches in the gently flowing river, shimmered and murmured in the water, providing a very dramatic symmetrical effect. The bridge itself looked like melted honey in the morning sun, with the dressed stone arch rings and rubble spandrels that pierced each main pier. We walked onto the centre of the bridge where there was a plaque that made me smile. *It cost £6000 to build,* read the sign. Why would it need to say that, I thought?

The Tweed Bridges Trust had paid for it along with the repairs needed in 1900. A new parapet wall and concrete foundations, the plaque informed me.

Walking back, I noticed a large stone and the word "ENGLAND" embedded in it, whilst on the Scottish side of the bridge, there was only a rounded, simple buttress, that looked far more appealing and in keeping with the bridge.

We went to get some snacks and arrived at the Cornhill Village shop. It was a lovely village with its distinctive, St Helen's Church.

George remarked that The Collingwood Arms would be a great place for lunch. I agreed, it looked great but wondered if he was going to treat me to lunch or the other way round.

The rest of the morning was spent on the lower bank, painting.

It was a glorious time.

We had a well earned ploughman's lunch and a pint, and I did end up paying for both of us. Ah well!

By the time we had finished painting, the sun was already behind the trees and although it wasn't near to sunset, the light had gone, as had any warmth that we had enjoyed earlier.

"Time to be going!" George announced as he stood up and had his paints and pad already in his bag, before I had even tipped away my water, cleaned my brushes and got off my little stool.

We agreed to meet on Monday morning and I must admit I was glad that I would have the weekend to relax.

Chapter 5

The three of us had decided to go to the pub that night, although the best places were the hotel bars, and there weren't many of those.

It was a cold walk through TweedMouth and over the river. We turned right into Bridge Street and walked up and along Meg's Mount and over the road then somehow we ended up at the old disused Berwick Barracks. We had reached all these places by taking random turns and some steps up the side of MaryGate that lead us along the walls.

Finally, after much retracing of our steps we reached Hide Hill and The Kings Arms Hotel. It was a busy Friday night and the bar there was full.

Rick went to buy the beers whilst Jas and I looked around for some seats.

In the corner was a small group of locals, about our age, so we settled into the sofa next to them.

As we waited for Rick, we listened to the conversation next to us. The group of local young people were in the Berwick Rowing Club and had just finished an evening's practice row. They were complaining about the strength of the tide. Although they were mainly guys, there was a dark haired, blue eyed young woman amongst them, with a dimpled smile. Jas had smiled at her and caught her eye and she was smiling back at him, not me. This was totally understandable as he was a good looking man and obviously attracted women easily. The guy next to her, probably her boyfriend, was too engrossed in discussing sculling techniques with the other crew members, to notice.

The interruption came when Rick arrived with our pints of amber gold beer, which allowed us to celebrate our new found comradeship and an exciting new period in our lives. It wasn't long before Rick struck up a conversation with one of the rowers. He had a knack, it turned out, of starting conversations with total strangers anywhere, which he appeared to have done all his life, many of them leading to numerous exciting encounters. So he kept reminding us!

"So, high there," Rick said, interrupting the guy next to him. "I heard you talking about sculling up the river."

The young guy had thick curly hair and beard, and was dressed like a local country gentleman. with his checked shirt and a tartan waistcoat. His sleeves were rolled up and his brown eyes stared at Rick with a steady gaze.

It was obvious that Rick's accent was not local, which had caught the attention of the others, stopping their conversations about tidal flow and sculling techniques, as each turned, and one by one focused on Rick.

"You an oarsman then?" The tartan waistcoat said.

"I have a traditional Native Indian canoe at home, in Canada and learnt how to paddle it on my lake outside Montreal. On my travels I have had some awesome times scooting down various rivers in Africa and Brazil." Said Rick, with raised eyebrows, that the group of men staring at him took it for a smug reply, rather than an informative discussion point.

"So you're a wee yankee paddler then?" One, particularly hard and thickly set, aggressive looking, ginger headed rower, interjected.

A sudden tension rose in the beer filled air, and it was quite palpable.

"Hey, maybe I can buy you all a beer, and we can talk about your rowing club. It would be amazing to do some *rowing* here?" Rick said loudly, making sure that they all heard him, especially the young man with the ginger hair.

Rick's offer of beer had magically done the trick and lowered the temperature immediately, albeit at a high price. He struggled to get to his feet and stood with his hands in his pockets while he took their orders, before disappearing through the crowd to the bar.

This left me talking to the tartan waistcoat, and Jas, teeth shining, starting up a conversation with the good looking young woman with the dimpled smile, as the rest of the group restarted their previous conversations.

"Sorry about that," I immediately found myself saying as a form of apology for Rick's rather robust, self introduction.

"We have just arrived here. I'm painting with one of your local water colour artists and these two are staying with me for a while. It's so beautiful up here. I'm renting a small cottage on the other side of the river." I said, realising that I was talking for the sake of it and giving more information than was necessary.

The tartan waistcoat stuck out his hand for me to shake. It was an intentionally strong, firm grip, but was a sign of acceptance and friendship as well, I thought.

"My name's Howard." He said with a refined Border accent. "And you are?"

"Oh, err. I'm Peter and this is Jas. The other chap, the Canadian, is Rick."

"Aye, well good to meet you all. So you're a painter and decorator?" He mused, with a grin. "I own the Baxter Estate, above TweedMouth, which is on the other side of the river, above where you are. I'm looking for an odd job man." He spoke quietly when he said this, but with a purposeful tone.

"Oh, I'm not that sort of painter. I paint landscapes with watercolours and oils." I replied, behaving and sounding like I had just been stamped on.

A big smile came across Howard's face as he turned to the rest of the group.

"Hey, guys. We have a wee painter chap here. Come up to see us and paint our brilliant countryside and stuff."

I could feel several pairs of eyes suddenly start to drill into me and heard the occasional hint of a laugh emerge from one or two.

"So who is the local painter that you are working with? We will probably know him, if he is local and any good."

"His name's George Bellingham." I said hesitantly, wondering whether there would be more mirth to develop.

To my very pleasant surprise, it was the woman with the dimple smile that spoke out straight away.

"Well, well. That's truly wonderful. So you are the young artist that is going to be working with my uncle for his Summer Exhibition. I hear you are a terrific painter. My uncle says you are *almost* as good as him," she enthused.

"My name is Elizabeth Bellingham. He's my dad's brother and very well thought of around here."

The whole group atmosphere changed immediately.

"Your Uncle, Liz!" Said Howard.

His bright piercing eyes hadn't left my face and now he had a big and extremely pleasant grin on his bearded face.

"He is considered to be an artist of distinction in the Borders, and has almost a princely status here," Howard continued, still smiling. "You must do a painting of my humble house," he continued with enthusiasm and with a look of pride and amazement on his face, as if he had just won the national lottery. "I will of course pay you for it." He added, as an afterthought.

"Perhaps I could come and see your *humble house* next week and we can discuss what aspect would be appropriate." I said, as I felt my heart racing with both relief and a little pride.

"Call me Liz, and I am so pleased to meet you." Said my new found admirer and savour.

I just caught a very strange and dark look from Jas, as we all turned when Rick, muscling his way through the crowd, arrived balancing a tray of drinks. He looked quite comical with his glasses not quite sitting right on the bridge of his nose, the tip of his tongue sticking out between his teeth and several pints wobbling around on a tray, that had seen better days, as he walked towards us.

He made a big theatrical performance out of handing round the drinks, and probably thought, as the mood was now very upbeat, how clever he had been in defusing the situation.

Meanwhile, Jas had slumped back onto the sofa. The smile had gone and a heavy brooding look had settled on his brow.

We all introduced ourselves more formally, and sat in a huddle. Whilst some discussed rowing with Rick, I talked with a local historian, called Trevor, who was "in between" jobs and was studying Berwick's, long and divided military history, at the local library. He was a large, but sadly not a particularly muscular young man and his hair was thinning on the top of his head, which made him look a lot older than he was.

Jas seemed to have switched back into his happy self, when I looked over and found he was back in deep conversation with Liz again, who seemed quite besotted by this exotic, good looking and entertaining Indian, with his big smile and even bigger charm offensive.

Just before we realised it was almost closing time, Howard turned to me and asked if I played tennis.

"I have a court at the house, but none of these buggers ever want to play, as they know I'll beat them all. I might not be the best oarsman in Berwick, but I'm pretty good with a racket." His speech was a little slurred, but I realised it was a genuine challenge.

"Perhaps, Rick the Canoe, would like to join us too."

Rick heard the challenge, and as usual, enthusiastically nodded his agreement without hesitation, but before Howard could ask Jas, he saw Jas shaking his head.

"I don't play tennis, sorry man. Anyway, Liz has invited me to meet some of her pottery friends." He said with a smirk.

"Since when did you like pottery?" Rick shouted across at him. "That's the first I've heard that you were interested in anything, except screwing."

The rowing club guys suddenly stopped talking. Liz stopped smiling, but as she had drunk far too much, giggled instead.

The atmosphere had become strained again and so, taking Jas by the arm, whilst catching Rick's eye, I shuffled and struggling to get out of my seat to stand up with Jas, announced that we had a long walk back, but would see Howard and whoever else was up for a lesson in tennis, the following morning, at 'Baxter House'.

With that final gesture, the three of us managed to manoeuvre ourselves through the crowd to the hotel exit.

The cold, fresh air hit me, and my head started to spin. None of us spoke as we staggered back over the bridge and finally reached Crab Cottage, just before midnight.

We were all cold from our walk back, and whilst Rick and I decided to call it a night and go to bed, Jas, back in his strange dark mood, wanted to stay up and watch TV.

The beer and fresh air had brought on a great need to sleep and with that, we left Jas in the lounge, watching a film.

The sunlight shattered on the water, shedding streaks of brilliant crystal slivers across the waves rolling swollen on the beach outside the cottage. I watched the screaming seagulls through my window when I finally woke up properly. My head hurt and my mouth felt dry, like old sandpaper.

Over the picket fence, across the sand I watched an old man struggle against the wind, with his dog.

Staggering into the kitchenette, I put the kettle on to make tea, when Rick heard me and had dressed, before joining me. He wore long baggy shorts and an old T-shirt, which made me laugh.

"Is that what you are going to wear to play tennis in?" I enquired.

"Hey man, what's so funny. These are vintage," he said, grabbing the bottoms of his shorts and grinning, as usual.

"Besides I didn't come here with clothes, to play tennis in." He said, looking a little hurt at my comments and mirth.

"I was thinking," he said, still with his pretend hurt look on his unshaven face. "I wonder if there is anyone who has got a scuba diving business here?"

He sat down at the table, and placing his glasses on the top of his head, started to scour the local newspaper he had bought the day before, looking for any adverts.

"There is an old wreck in the docks here and it would be awesome to go take a look down there." He muttered as he strained to read the advertisement section.

"We could ask Howard, when we see him?" I suggested, not really taking him too seriously. "He will know for sure, or if not then one of the other guys from the Rowing Club will definitely know of a Diving Club, if there is one."

We left Jas still asleep, got in the Land Rover and set off towards TweedMouth to try and find "Baxter Estate".

"Can we just have a walk on the walls first." Rick asked.

"Sure, we haven't really seen them since we arrived, well not in daylight." I mused, looking at my watch. We didn't have too much time, but we weren't too worried if we ended up being a little late.

Rick wanted a bit of sea air, so we parked under the walls at Northgate first, and decided to do the Seawalk on the walls. The tide was out, and apart from the occasional dog walker, nobody else was there. The town's fortifications were indeed quite magnificent, and so we continued along to Lowick Bastion with its wide thick walls. I looked at the gentle grassy slopes and the heavy fortifications at each corner, where we could look down into a courtyard, where a 17th century mounted cannon stood by a hidden opening. We took the walk back across the golf course and half way across, I turned to see the huge expanse of the Lowick Bastion, with the church spire, just behind and a hint of the Bell Tower to its right. George had suggested we should paint there. It was a place I needed to sketch first, but when it was a little warmer, and probably, when the trees in the background were fully open, I would return to paint it with him.

Howard had given some directions, although they had been a little vague, the night before. He had been rather drunk, so we weren't sure where we were going to end up.

Luckily, as there wasn't much of TweedMouth to get lost in, we arrived at the huge gates just off the main road heading south along the A1. We were a little later than we had agreed, but didn't really care too much.

There was a stone, carved sign that announced we had arrived at the right place.

"Awesome. This is some estate." Rick drawled as we drove through the tall, open gates.

A long, tarmac road, wound round some spruce trees and large laurel bushes, before opening up to a wide expanse of lawns. There, in front of us stood a beautiful red sandstone Georgian manor house. Although it had seen better days, it still looked magnificent and was certainly more than Rick and I had been expecting.

A big blue Mercedes, four wheel drive SUV, sat on the driveway. It was parked badly, at a strange angle.

"Howard, didn't drive back home last night, did he?" I asked Rick, staring at the Mercedes, before turning to see Rick's inquisitive look and raised eyebrows.

"How else would his Merc beast be here?" Rick said, giving me a sideways look and another raised eyebrow.

We stood, ringing the bell on the side of the oversized front door. We waited and then rang the bell a few more times before it slowly opened. Howard, his hair sticking up as if he had just received a thousand volts through it, peered round the door, his eyes half closed.

"What the fuck," he said, "what the hell time is this?"

"I don't think he's pleased to see us," Rick said, with a chuckle and his head swaying from side to side. "Perhaps he didn't mean today."

"Or perhaps, he didn't mean *any* day." I added, as I took a step back and was ready to turn away and head back to the Land Rover. "You did say, last night, we would be playing tennis this morning." I questioned, trying to make light of his seeming indignation.

"I did indeed," he growled, "but when I said morning, I didn't mean this bloody early."

"Gee Howard, it has gone ten o'clock, and we have already been for a walk on the walls and thought we were late." Rick pleaded with him, trying to sound reasonable, but actually sounding like he was scolding him.

"Fuck you two," Howard said though gritted teeth. "Let me get dressed and I will take you both on, and give you a tennis lesson to remember."

He called us in, as he stumbled along the dark hall and up an oak staircase, disappearing into one of the rooms above, slamming the door behind him.

We shut the door and stood waiting. There were two large framed oil paintings of stern looking old men, hanging on opposite walls. There was an obvious familiarity in the faces.

"Probably his grandfather and great grandfather." Rick whispered to me as he caught me gazing up at them, whilst he strained to do the same.

Jas had finally rolled out of bed later that morning. He showered, trimmed his beard, made a coffee and scrambled some eggs, sprinkling a little coriander and cumin on to add some flavour.

He ate in silence, as he wondered how he was going to learn about making pots. He wanted to impress Liz, but he wasn't thinking just about pottery.

Turning on the radio, he found a music station that was playing his favourite music. Rock from the 70's. The beat had woken him up fully and he started to dance around the lounge singing whilst considering how to make his move on Liz.

As the music continued, his movements got a little wilder and his eyes a little brighter. A big smile split across his face as it had many times before. A broad, dangerous smile as he nodded and wagged his head, his thick black curls dancing with his moves.

It was an old Kink's song, "You really got me":

> Girl, you really got me goin'
> You got me goin' so I can't sleep at night…

He was happy enough to sing the chorus as he swirled and clapped and cheered to the heavy guitar riffs, jumping up and down in the small cottage lounge, whilst working on a plan of action in his mind.

46

Howard beat Rick and I, four games to two, then, sweating profusely, declared himself the winner and marched off the court, taking the rackets he had lent us with him, like trophies. As he disappeared round a yew hedge he shouted instructions for us to gather up the balls and join him for lunch in the Orangery, at the back of the house.

Despite his earlier physical state, he was certainly fitter than Rick and I, and even more annoying, was easily better at tennis than both of us put together.

When Rick and I found our way into the Orangery, Howard was sitting in a wicker chair, smoking a cigarette and blowing the blue smoke through the side of his mouth.

A rush of irrational resentment seized me. I was almost angry that he smoked and was still fitter than me, and that he had this huge, rambling, crumbling mansion.

He raised his left eyebrow in a high arch as he said, challenging me.

"I do like a good game of tennis, Peter. Oh, and while you are looking around my house, there isn't a day that goes by that I wish I had enough money to stop the roof from leaking when it rains, or the plumbing from leaking when it freezes."

An elderly woman came in, carrying a small tray of drinks. She stood close to Howard, staring unselfconsciously at Rick and I. We stared back at her just as intently and as I realised it was probably his mother. I was struck by how similar they were in that instant moment, the son with his mother. Both had expressive mouths and eyes that gleamed and the same grave look, yet full of naughty humour.

"Thank you mother, for the drinks. We certainly need them."

He gave me a quick smile as his mother served us all.

"So, tell me, did you enjoy the game this morning guys? Have you ever played tennis before?" He asked us, with a rather gleeful smile.

"Played before?" Rick frowned. "Of course, but we were obviously a little rusty."

"I haven't played for ages." I interrupted, trying to make my excuses.

"Actually, it was enjoyable beating you both at once, but with practice you will get better." He sighed.

His mother returned with the tray again, this time with a round of salmon sandwiches, which she presented to us with a solemn sense of ceremony. I expected Howard to eat his meal straight away, but he placed his plate back on the tray, lit another cigarette and laid back in his chair.

I was sitting on a straight backed chair which hurt my back, as I watched Howard lounge on his green velvet cushions in his wicker seat.

We finished our sandwiches and I was ready to leave.

"I don't suppose there is a scuba or diving club in Berwick, is there?" Rick said nonchalantly, looking at the distant clouds, out through the dirty windows of the Orangery.

"So, why do you want to know?"

"Oh, I just happen to have done an awful lot of scuba diving and heard there is a wreck worth seeing. Have you been scuba diving before, Howard?"

"Scuba diving, hey laddie? Well, there could be, but I'm not sure. I know a guy with a diving bell, with a helmet and suit, you know the kind?" He mocked.

"Wow, that would be awesome, but I've never done that before."

"Well, I will ask him and see what he says."

"Oh, Okay, then." Rick replied, with a little trepidation in his voice.

"No, you are welcome, if I can come too. It would be really great to see you go down."

"Okay, then," Rick said slowly, and then looked at me. "This will be awesome." I replied, shaking my head in a resigned shrug.

Howard's chest swelled with pride, and with a vaguely suspicious laugh, furrowed his brow as he stood up to see us out.

Chapter 6

It was a few days later when Jas had arranged to meet up with Liz. He had been reading a few articles on pottery and especially *throwing clay*.

I found it quite amusing that he thought that, just by reading up about it, would make him an expert suddenly, but then there are many people that believe that just by reading a lot about a subject entitles them to be an expert, or even having a critical opinion without having even tried to actually make something themselves.

The arrogance of people like that has always annoyed me. Even if something isn't very good, I think anyone who tries to make, or design, or write something, makes their efforts worth ten times that of those who just talk and criticise others who have actually produced something, that will always remain as their legacy.

"So, you are going to be a potter, Jas?" Rick enquired, with a grin and a chuckle.

"Yes, I am," he exclaimed, not raising his head up from the article he was reading. "Place the clay firmly on the Bat with the point facing down, get the wheel turning slowly and tap the clay ball to centre it, then ..." Jas said before I interrupted him.

"I think you might find it easier to read about it than to do it," I said smiling too. "Although I do admire your intentions. If that actually means you want to make something, like a real pot or plate."

"As opposed to just getting off with Liz!" Rick added, leaning over him, raising his glasses onto the top of his head as he did, in order to read the article as well.

We all met up at the King's Arms Hotel that night. The rowing crew were there, and greeted us, by waving their empty pint glasses our way as we entered.

It was obvious that they still thought Rick owed them at least another round or two. Liz was there, and waved at Jas. He danced over to her and gleefully sat down and immediately started to talk about pottery making, which seemed to impress her from the start.

I left them to talk and noticed Howard in his usual corner, arms stretched out across the back of the sofa behind his mates. He raised an arm in acknowledgement and continued his deep conversation with the guys on either side of him. I found a table and sat facing the group, waiting for Rick to arrive with the beers. He did eventually, after what seemed an age.

"Sorry guys. Long queue." He exclaimed loudly, in order to be heard over the noise of a full and heated discussion, by a group of men at the bar.

As he handed out the drinks, Howard called to him.

"Hey, Rick, come over and meet Angus," He hollered, waving his hand to beacon him over. "Angus, this is the

Canadian canoe guy who wants to go down to the wreck."
He said, shouting into Angus' left ear.

Rick handed them the beers and squeezed in alongside them both.

"You've been in a wee bell suit before?" Angus enquired in a heavy Borders accent.

"No, but I am a qualified scuba diver, so I guess I can manage to go down in a bell suit easily enough." Rick was absolutely awe struck. "To see the wreck, would be awesome." He said, with a huge emphasis on his favourite word.

I sat sipping my pint, and watched as Rick got into a deep conversation with Howard and his new found diving instructor as well as Jas and Liz talking, I assumed, about pottery, and throwing clods of clay around.

As I looked at Jas' face, I noticed a strange glint in his half closed eyes and his hand that was now resting suggestively on Liz's knee, slowly squeezing it. I felt the hairs on the back of my neck rise and a shudder run down my spine. It wasn't that I was jealous, on the contrary, but it was the look that he was giving her that I found strangely scary.

She didn't seem to mind at all though.

The rest of the rowing team, pint glasses being emptied rapidly, were all getting well inebriated, whilst I sat alone at my table, wondering what to do next.

I needn't have worried, as at that moment, Trevor, the historian chap that we had met the previous week, burst into the bar. He stormed over to the group, red cheeked and wide eyed. I thought he had won the lottery as his coat hanger smile got wider when he saw me.

None of the group had really noticed him, let alone his radiant smiling face, so he sat down next to me. He was breathing deeply and could hardly speak. He was so excited.

"Well, hello Trevor. You look happy," I said, turning to him, wondering if he would like me to buy him a pint.

"What are you so pleased about?"

"You won't believe this," he managed to say, gasping with every word."Berwick is at war with Russia!!!"

Despite the raucous chatter in the bar, everyone heard Trevor and suddenly the room fell silent. All eyes turned to stare in disbelief at him, sitting there still grinning.

"What the fuck, Trevor?" Howard said, being the first to break the strange silence.

"Have you been eating those magic mushrooms again?"

The group at the bar all laughed and started up their heated and stupid arguments about football player's salaries and corrupt, rich club owners, especially Russian ones.

They all turned and sneered at Trevor when that was mentioned.

"No, I mean Howard. Berwick is officially still at war with Russia." He was waving his arms about and staring wide eyed at Howard.

I asked him if he wanted a pint. I got no reply, but looking at the bead of sweat on his brow and the colour of his red cheeks, I guessed he needed one and got up to go to the bar. I was waiting to be served when I felt someone standing very close behind me. I turned to find Jas standing up close against my back.

"Getting the drinks in are you, Peter?" He said quietly over my shoulder.

He was so close behind me that I could smell his beery breath, in my nostrils. That same scary feeling rose up in me as did the hairs on the back of my neck again. I couldn't turn round as he was so close and I was hemmed in on both sides by others, waiting to be served.

"Get a pint for me and a vodka and tonic for my Liz, will you. There's a good chap?"

I couldn't see the red in his eyes, but I knew they were burning into the back of my head, as I nodded and hailed the waiter again.

I got back to the table with the tray of drinks just as Trevor was explaining about what he had found in the library archives that evening.

The whole group seemed to have suddenly sobered up and instead of mocking him, were straining to listen to what he had to say about his findings in the old chronicles.

"I was just reading through some old newspapers and found an article, written in 1914, about Berwick still being at War.

So, I thought, this is strange," he continued, hunched over his knees with us all straining to hear him. "I thought they were talking about the First World War, but it turns out it was about the Crimean War." His voice became more excited.

"What are you on about?" Howard said.

"That was in the middle of the 1850's."

"Exactly," Trevor continued. "The Crimean war, as you all know, was a military conflict between 1853 and 1856.

Russia lost to an alliance between France, the then Ottoman Empire and the United Kingdom."

"Ah yes," I said."The battle of Balaclava. 1854 I think. Part of the siege of Sevastopol." I mused, feeling rather pleased with remembering some history from my school days.

"Charge of the Light Brigade. The 650 men on their horses and all that." Howard added, giving me a wink. "I remember my history too, Peter."

"So, what's all this got to do with Berwick?" Rick chimed in.

Trevor gave him a wizened look and continued. Everyone was mesmerised with the story, but also possibly, from the effects of the beer.

"It was all about Christian minorities in Palestine, when it was part of the Ottoman Empire." Trevor was suddenly stopped.

"Oh, do get on with it, Trev. What's Berwick got to do with it?" Angus said, folding his arms and blowing a long sigh as he did. Trevor was beginning to lose the excitement of the others.

"Okay, this is the good bit. You see, Queen Victoria signed the declaration in 1853. It said - *Victoria Queen of Great Britain, Ireland, Berwick upon Tweed and the British Dominions beyond the seas.*" Trevor stopped for a moment as he remembered more before he carried on. "But, Berwick wasn't mentioned in the Treaty of Paris that concluded the Crimes War in 1856." He was almost shouting and looked quite manic as he raised both arms in utter joy.

"So, fucking what?" Howard screamed back.

"Well, that means that, technically, we, that means us in Berwick, are technically still at war with Russia." Trevor said and sighed. He leant back in his chair and took a very long drink of his beer.

"Bloody hell. Why was Berwick named as a separate place?" One of the rowing crew asked.

"I think it goes back to 1482. Do you know Berwick has exchanged hands between England and Scotland, I think 14 times." Trevor said, trying to remember the exact number.

"Aye, And Berwick Rangers football club is actually over the border in bloody Scotland, when it should be in the English league." One of the men at the bar said as he threw in the additional piece of information.

Howard was quite intrigued by this sudden revelation.

"So, Berwick, at that time, was neither in Scotland nor in England!" He said, and stroked his chin.

"Exactly, and most certainly a possibility." Trevor said gleefully, as he finished his pint.

"I'm going to write a letter to the *Berwick Advertiser* in the morning, and ask them to investigate it further. I'm also going to write to the Russian Embassy and demand an immediate ceasefire." He finally said, before standing up proudly and disappearing into the throng at the bar to get another pint.

The general feelings for the rest of that night were ones of mirth, disbelief and drunken bravado.

Shouts of *"We'll all be prisoners of war in Moscow, this time tomorrow,"* were the last few words I heard, before leaving with Rick for our usual walk over the bridge back to Spittal.

The tide was out and the river therefore very low. We chose to walk along the walls a little way and I gazed over at the twinkling lights, that was Spittal. It had never been the prettiest of places and yet with all the lights twinkling from the cottages up from the waters edge, it did have some charm. I looked and found Jas before leaving. He was drunk and totally engrossed in groping Liz, but I did catch his eye, for a second. The smile left his face when he saw my gaze, then he gave me a drunken one finger and turned back to Liz.

Two days later, as I walked to the cafe to meet with George for another day's painting, I passed the newsagents shop. In the front window was the *Berwick Advertiser's* headline.

"Russian Gun Boat Expected Up the Tweed"

I couldn't help but laugh and muttered, *well done you, Trevor,* under my breath as I entered the cafe to buy George and I breakfast, as usual.

It was a gorgeously warm day and I was looking forward to working with George in a new location on yet another scene on the banks of the river, this time locally in Berwick. I recounted Trevor's story to George and we both laughed, although I did notice he looked carefully at every distant boat that came into view from around the bend in the river.

"We must go and paint at North Bay," George suddenly announced, stroking his chin. "There is the sea wall there with a little ancient beacon at the end.

It almost looks like a harbour with that sea wall on its right side and a stony spit on its left. Good sunset may be." He was talking to himself I thought, but he was obviously thinking of places I would enjoy painting.

"Then there is a lovely wee view of the Berwick coast line from, what's called the Northumbrian Bastion, here on the walls of the town. The walls curve round to the right and beyond are two rows of cottages, with their slate roofs and chimney stacks. Behind them is the sea and a gorgeous sweeping beach and low cliffs," he said, sighing gently. "Makes for a good wee painting, I think you'll find. Another day though."

Chapter 7

Rick met up with Angus that morning too, down by the docks where the wreck of an old sailing barge could be found, having been sunk in a storm a couple of hundred years before.

They had agreed to dive, as long as the weather was good. It was going to be high tide late morning and so would be perfect timing.

He was waiting for him in his old van and had already got out a shiny battered, brass helmet and a rather suspect old diving suit and a pair of heavy leaded boots.

As Rick strode over to him, Angus was bent, inside the back of the van, dragging out a reel of hoses to be attached to the helmet and an air pump that wouldn't have looked out of place in a museum.

He hadn't noticed Rick at first, until he heard his booming Canadian voice.

"Awesome, man," he said, his eyes wide open with glee and picking up the old suit. "Am I supposed to fit into this diving suit?"

"Of course, you wee girlie. You're not that big. Get those clothes off, and I trust you have some bathers. A rash vest might go down well too, but I have one in the van that will fit you, if you don't." Angus stood up, hands on his hips and winked at Rick, as he eyed him up and down for size.

Angus fitted one end of the hoses to the helmet and the other to his pumping machine. It needed someone to turn the wheel and keep turning it so that there was a constant and sufficient flow of air. He saw Rick's look of amazement, but managed to convince him that it would all work out just fine.

An hour later, having climbed down the rungs of the ladder into the cold black water, breathing heavily and feeling the weight of the lead boots, Rick stood on the sea bottom next to the wreck. Through the murky dark green, he could just make out the shape of the limpet encrusted hull of the broken barge and was inching his way along the side, when he had to stop abruptly.

He suddenly found that he couldn't breath very well.

He started to feel dizzy and found it difficult to stand up straight.

He turned round, confused, but just managed to stomp his way back to the ladder as the air in the helmet got hotter and the level of carbon dioxide built up. He tried to stay calm and breathe more slowly, but he found he was panicking more with each sluggish step.

He couldn't think straight anymore and a dark fog was beginning to cloud his mind as he struggled with every step. He put his foot on the first rung and looking up he could just see light above him as he climbed, ever slower towards the surface. Reaching the top rung, he collapsed head first onto the harbour wall and frantically unscrewed the big brass nuts to get the face mask open. A rush of cold fresh air made him gasp as he swung open the caged glass front.

He could breathe again and took in several deep breaths of glorious sea air as he lay shaking with fear on the ground.

While he lay there, gasping, he looked over to the wheel of the hand pump. The handles swung gently back and forth, but Angus was nowhere to be seen.

"What the fuck?" Rick managed to say, still breathing deeply, his hands still shaking as he struggled with the helmet.

He tried to shout, but little came out of his gaping mouth, then all went black.

He didn't know how long he had been out, but when he came too and opened his eyes, the helmet had been removed and he was lying on his back with a face staring down at him.

Angus was shouting something at him and as he blinked awake, and slowly the voice became louder and the face became clearer.

He had Rick by the shoulders, trying to revive him.

Blood was running down the side of Angus' now pale face. Rick looked into his red rimmed eyes. The look was wild. The furrowed brow and clotted blood in his hair, made for a scary picture as Rick's eyes finally focused.

"Christ, I'm so happy you are okay, man." Angus said, breathlessly, deeply shocked and obviously in pain.

He sat down next to Rick and held a bloodied cloth to the back of his head. He had a grimace look on his face that moved between anger and pain, fear and relief.

Rick managed to sit up. He still had the suit on, but not the heavy boots.

"What the hell happened?" Rick finally managed to say, still not sure what was going on. He had a throbbing headache, but guessed Angus did too, so didn't mention it.

"You had just gone down and I watched you disappear into the depth and was keeping a close eye on you and maintaining the rhythm, turning the wheel steadily to keep the air flow constant. Once you were down it just needed me to watch the pressure dial so that I could ensure your air supply was even." Angus spoke quickly while still trying to stem the flow of blood.

"I suddenly couldn't breathe." Rick said, looking at him incredulously. "Why did you stop pumping and what happened to your fucking head?"

"Someone smacked me from behind with that lobster pot." He said, turning to point at the large netted wooden cage by the van.

"He knocked me out cold for a wee while. I came too, blood everywhere. There was nobody around except you lying face down on the dock side, at the top of the ladder."

They were both still dazed and shaking as two fishermen came running over. Angus was the priority and as Rick sat on the edge of the harbour wall, he looked over at the bridge.

There were a few people standing watching, but what caught his eye was the figure of an Indian man leaning nonchalantly on the central parapet, staring at him with a hard, cold expression on his face.

He looked like Jas, but as he hadn't put his glasses back on yet, the image was a little blurred, so he wasn't sure.

Rick waved to get his attention.

The man didn't wave back but instead, turned and walked on along the bridge in the opposite direction. Perhaps he was mistaken then, after all.

As Rick struggled to rid himself of the diving suit, an ambulance arrived. One of the fishermen had called 999, even though Angus had insisted he was fine and there was no need for them. He was more concerned when the police arrived. It occurred to Rick that perhaps diving in the harbour, without permission, was not quite as legal as he had thought.

The most concerning problem was who had knocked Angus unconscious and even more so, why?

Rick was given oxygen and then they were taken off to hospital. Angus needed to have a couple of stitches in his head before both were questioned by the local constabulary.

Before the sun had set, I had dropped George off and was back at Crab Cottage trying to decide how to prepare the salmon that some friend of George's had kindly given me. It was large and fresh, but I didn't know where to start. I was in the kitchen looking at it wondering how to begin, when in walked Rick.

It took him a full fifteen minutes to explain the day's events in detail. We had sat out in the sandy garden facing the sea, with a cold beer each and a bag of cashew nuts each and hadn't heard the front door open or indeed Jas' silent footsteps as he approached them both sitting by the picket fence, listening to the waves and feeling the evening breeze. "What are you two talking about?" He said quietly, but firmly, as he stuck his head in-between them both.

I jumped a little in surprise, but relaxed as soon as I saw it was only Jas, and yet, the tone of his voice seemed questioningly harsh.

Rick's reaction surprised me much more when he stood and turned quickly, spilling his beer and dropping the bag of nuts. He seemed physically shaken at the sudden intrusion that broke our peaceful sea gazing, and his dramatic story.

What Rick had failed to mention, up until this moment, was that he thought he had seen Jas on the bridge, even though he agreed that perhaps, in the end, that he must have been mistaken.

"I waved at you this morning." Was all Rick said initially, expecting to find out whether it had indeed been him.

"Where was that?" Jas replied, not looking at either of us.

"I didn't see you. Where were you?"

"You were looking straight at me from the bridge," Rick sneered, half closing his eyes. "Don't tell me you didn't know it was me. The only fucking person to be diving in TweedMouth Harbour today. Everyone on the bridge was looking. Not surprisingly after what had happened." Rick was getting upset and angry.

"I have no idea what you are talking about. It obviously wasn't me or else I….." Jas's explanation was curtailed by Rick's angry response.

"I don't think there are many other fucking Indians in Berwick right this minute, Jas, and besides, you knew I was going diving, and where, so you must have walked right past the dock from the cottage, on your way to Berwick and over the old bridge." Rick was shouting now, right into Jas' face.

"You didn't stop to see me go into the water, did you, Jas?" he said, almost accusingly, as he continued getting more animated. "I don't suppose you had anything to do with the incident?"

"What the hell are you talking about, Rick, it wasn't me, I wasn't there?" Jas said, looking suddenly flustered. "And anyway, what incident?"

"Just as I was in the water and under the wreck, Angus was smashed unconscious and subsequently, I nearly suffocated - to death."

The conversation stopped suddenly when Jas just turned and left to go to his room. The silence left between us, was only broken by the sound of the waves and the evening wind as the sun set.

The salmon I was given, never saw the table that night, nor any other night.

I had been appalled at Rick's outburst and suggestion that Jas could have in any way been involved, and yet I felt very uneasy, as I sensed the same uncomfortable tingling down my spine and the stiffening hairs on the back of my neck, when Rick confronted him. It was the same sensation I had felt on seeing Jas with Liz, in the hotel bar.

Why did I feel like this? Why had it happened again?

There was something a little strange about Jas that made me feel uneasy around him, but I had no idea what it was or why?

It wasn't logical for me to think these thoughts as nothing had happened to suggest that something was amiss, and yet this latest incident raised more questions than answers, and besides, there was still the big question.

Who had knocked Angus unconscious and why?

Reading the *Berwick Advertiser* the following weekend was quite the highlight of the week, not only for us, but also for the whole town.

When we all met up with the rowing club group, it was all they wanted to talk about.

Rick and Angus were suddenly the celebrities of the moment. The dramatic, but illegal dive, a near death experience and the unexplained attack on poor Angus, that had left him bloodied and unconscious.

The column headline, on page three, this time, was very different from the previous week.

"An illegal dive nearly ends in tragedy."

The Police investigation into the affair had not come up with any conclusive evidence, but had suggested that it might have been local fishermen, unhappy with some foreign divers, perhaps treasure hunters illegally diving on a well known wreck, and had decided to take the matter upon themselves to stop it.

Well, that was what the columnist had written and the newspaper had printed anyway.

Angus and Howard, who were both reading the article out loud, as Rick, Jas and I entered the bar, both said.

"No fucking way."

"We know all the fishermen and they know us too and nobody, but nobody in Berwick would take this sort of action." Howard bellowed, screaming his outrage and disapproval across the whole bar.

All the others were in agreement, as in fact were most of the local population it seemed, after hearing the other people's accounts in the bar, as to what might have happened.

"I have a few alternative thoughts though," Rick suddenly said that stopped the noisy banter, "but as I have no proof, then maybe the police investigation report is right."

His words sounded hard and his thoughts didn't go down well with the others as if he was implying they were perhaps involved in some way.

Rick felt all eyes were on him as he spoke.

"Hey, no, none of you guys!" He said, horrified at the way it must have sounded and offered to get the next round in.

With that he sat down next to Angus to inspect his stitched head and accepted the admiration of the rowing team along with a large order from the group.

I sat at my usual table as Jas looked around, obviously and eagerly, hunting for Liz.

Howard started to ask Rick about the police interrogation he had undergone that morning. They had given, both he and Angus, a heavy questioning that had culminated in a warning about illegal diving in the harbour.

"So the police will have you on file. Are you going to keep it quiet or shall we write to the *Berwick Advertiser*?" He enquired, getting a laugh from the rest.

"Young divers harassed over innocent diving." Howard said in a loud local brogue, waving his arms in the air as if he were writing the next headline for the newspaper.

"Well, everyone else seems to be getting into the news these days," Angus added, looking over at a smiling Trevor. Angus stopped, and grinned at Trevor until the grin became a playful laugh.

He wore a tweed waistcoat over his white cotton shirt. In his heavy, black jeans that were coated in engine oil, and despite his ordeal and an obvious aching head, he was cool, almost as cool as he looked.

"Did you ever get that letter written, Trevor?" he laughed."You would have thought the Berwick Council might have had something to say! It was the greatest thing I ever heard, until our story." He shouted, smiling at Rick.

"Yes, I did and you know I did. I am waiting to hear from the Russian Embassy, in London, I'll have you know."

"My story managed to get on the inside pages of a National Newspaper, I'll have you know, mate." Trevor mused again, this time folding his arms and sitting back with a smug smile on his shiny red face.

Howard leant forward to take up the story again.

"So where was I? I'm losing it today, man. Oh yeah, the police interrogation and having you on file. They would have wanted to do some checking on you. So they asked you loads of questions, like where you were from, why you were here and who knocked Angus out?"

"But the police weren't interested in who smacked Angus." Rick said, a little annoyed, whilst trying to understand Howard's point.

"No, man, they were checking up on you, to find out who would want to fuck *you* over, then, send you back to Canada to get you off their files. Just remember, you were the one that would have suffocated to death had you not got out of the water in time. I'm telling you Rick, it had nothing to do with the dive. I think someone wanted you dead."

Rick's eyes widened in surprise, and then narrowed into a concerned frown. He lifted his pint to his lips and sipped it, slowly.

I, too, was becoming a little worried at Howard's scary theory and accusations. For some reason I found myself watching Jas. He was sitting next to Liz but his hooded gaze was focused on the trio on the sofa.

Rick sat in stunned silence and I reached out to put my hand on his shoulder.

He was right to be worried, of course. He had almost been suffocated to death, either through a stupid act of violence against Angus, or by an act of direct malice with intent to kill Rick.

Chapter 8

The loose windows rattled me awake early the following morning. It was still cold outside especially as the North wind blew straight across the beach and all the cottages that ran along the same shore line. I opened the thin curtains, and to my surprise, saw Rick struggling to pick up driftwood from the beach. We liked the orange flames that the salty wood gave us, burning brightly in the log burner.

"It's the Sodium in the salt, you know." He would say, every time.

The sea was rough and I could see the sand was whipping into his eyes and mouth. I knocked on the window pane, but he couldn't hear me through the howl of the wind and the crashing of the waves.

As I put the kettle on to make some tea, a sharp cold burst of air hit me. It was Rick, slamming the back door closed, as he came in with his cargo of wood. He broke up the longer pieces and tossed all of them into the basket with the rest of the logs, wiped his nose with the back of his hand and took his glasses off to wipe the lenses. They were covered in sea salt and had also fogged up, as the warmth from the kitchen hit them.

He squinted at me as he rubbed them clear.

"Man, it's freaking cold out there. And that wind! What's with the weather here? It's supposed to be Springtime for goodness sake."

We both laughed as I handed him a cup of steaming tea and sat him down at the old kitchen table.

There was a small silence, before finally, Rick spoke.

"So, Jas left early this morning?" He asked, knowing the answer. An unusual rhetorical question from him, I thought. He is usually quite direct.

"He's meeting up with Liz and they are joining up with her pottery friends. I gather he is - having a go - today." I said, with a hint of cynicism.

Rick just looked at me, and then at his mug of tea before changing the subject.

"Do you want to go to this Rowing Club event at the Yacht Club this evening? Angus invited us. It starts about five, once they have finished varnishing one of their boats, or something. Meeting up afterwards is probably just an excuse to get drunk, but then what else is there to do around here."

I wasn't sure whether he was really interested or not, but it *was* at the Berwick Yacht Club, which was quite upmarket for Berwick.

His lack of enthusiasm had seemed a little out of character, but then he had done very little since he and Jas arrived. Neither of them seemed in a hurry to move on anywhere else.

"I thought the whole point of you coming up to Northumberland was to find out about your ancestors. I think you said they came from Middlesbrough, or somewhere close by?" I suggested, hoping that I might gain some insight as to any future plans he might have about moving on, or at least doing some research about his grandfather whilst still living with me.

"I did think that's where they were from and I did go to find out. Actually, Trevor got me into the library and I researched my family history from there. Turns out they came from Goathland. It's a village in the Scarborough district of North Yorkshire, up on the North York Moors in the National Park." He said, taking off his glasses and rubbing his eyes. He looked tired.

"I think you'll find it's probably closer to Whitby. It used to have a steam railway. The North Yorkshire Moors Railway." I recalled slowly, not that Rick seemed particularly interested.

I wasn't sure how I knew this, but there wasn't much point in continuing to ask him any more.

"The police said that it was local fishermen." Rick suddenly said, that caught me by surprise.

"The newspaper said the same thing. I could have died!"

"You don't think that's true, do you?" I asked, questioningly.

"I fear that I don't," he sighed, suddenly and uncharacteristically solemn again. "They didn't think I was just the pipes blocked or that Angus had just suddenly stopped pumping, either. Someone knocked him out. Howard, may be right."

"Do you think you know who it was?"

"Yes, I believe I do. "

"Do you know why this person might have tried to kill you?" I asked gently, not really thinking who he had in mind.

"No, not at all, which is what perplexes me so much, but more importantly, will they try again?"

"Who would want to do such a thing?"

"I suspect one of the rowing crew."

"The *rowing crew*, for fuck's sake!" I gasped! My mouth gaped open, and my gaze drifted on the tide of my thoughts.

"Rick - I'll get you another cuppa."

I strode into the kitchen, put the kettle on and read the newspaper article again while the kettle boiled. I read the journalist's column, every word. I was drawn to a different conclusion. I felt a sense of solidarity and kinsmanship with Rick, I wanted to find out and then understand the real story.

"Here Rick, tea, milk, no sugar." I said, handing him the mug.

Rick pouted his lower lip, and offered a flourish of his hand to dismiss the distressing subject. The gesture was weak and his head lolled forward, and he stared vacantly at the table in front of him.

"I can't believe it. It is simply not believable. Why would *anyone* want me dead?"

I ambled to the back door and looked out across the grey thrashing waves and whipped up white crests, and let my thoughts wander while I listened to Rick's plaintive explanations and questions. Selfishly, I wondered first what the *incident* might mean for me and Jas, as we too were, no doubt considered - outsiders, and might be subject to being attacked. I wasn't sure that anyone who wasn't born and bred in the Borders, weren't considered as unwelcome beings. If you were seen to be from further south or even worse, from overseas, perhaps it would be a reason to spill a little blood. But that was insane, as the only blood spilt was that of a local - Angus.

I glanced back at Rick. He smiled at me weakly, tilting his head on one side. It was a heartbreaking smile, and his eyes were inflamed with unshed tears. He was afraid, and yet still he smiled, to comfort me maybe, to reassure me, to include me in his bewildered concerns.

We were silent, for a while, the two of us, lost in our speculation and worry.

Then Rick spoke.

"I think I have another thought for you." He said softly, wrenching me back into the moment once more.

Jas had left the cottage early. He was meeting Liz over in the town and from there they would meet up with members of the local Potter's Society. They had a studio on the West side of the walls and several, albeit not very good, but creative and enthusiastic members.

When they walked into the studio, his eyes fixed on a beautiful young woman, a friend of Liz's. Every kind of, would be potter and artistic hobby crafters were there. It depressed Jas, like the first sight of the slums of India he remembered as a boy, but as Liz led him in and introduced him to the group, he laughed and smiled and everyone took to him straight away, as they always did.

Liz was stealing sideways glances at his face as they wandered through the studio.

"How are you liking our little studio?"

"I love it." He answered, and it was true. To his eyes, the little potter's studio was beautiful. It was romantic, but haphazard and neglected, crumbling and cold. The array of hand thrown pots were magnificent, he said. And there were more smiles in the eyes of those elderly artists than he had seen for a long time.

74

Yes, he was a *little* unnerved at the fact that they thought him a potter also, but they had yet to discover his amazing lack of talent and indeed disinterest in pottery and even less, in making any. He had only one thing on his mind, and it wasn't throwing pots or sculpting heads from cold wet clay.

It was as if he had found himself in a performance of some extravagant, complex drama, and he didn't have a script. But he smiled, and smiling was easy for Jas.

It was late afternoon and the wind had dropped a little and the sea had calmed, when Rick and I arrived at the steps leading up to the Berwick Yacht Club.

Howard had told us to be there early.

We obviously were early, as nobody else was there except a bored looking barman. The tide was on the turn, but not at all high enough to allow those out sailing to get back into the mouth of the river yet, so there were no hardened sailors in the club at that time.

However, it wasn't long before we heard a couple of cars arrive, followed by raucous laughing and loud voices. The rowing crew had arrived.

Rick and I were out on the veranda, overlooking the mouth of the river. The barman brought us our beers and slammed them down onto the table with reckless discretion. The service in the Yacht Club seemed to be either abrupt or hostile. The churlishness of the bar staff was legendary, Howard later explained.

"It's my favourite place in the whole world, to be treated like dirt." He had said when he and the boys were served in the same manner as we had been.

"A toast!" Angus declared, raising his glass to touch Rick's. "To illegal diving and be damned! Salut!"

We all drank half the contents from our glass tankards. Angus let out a loud sigh of pleasure, and then drank the rest. He was ordering a second when someone pointed to the fishermen who had been sitting on the shore line. Everyone turned to look at the sandbank to see several fishermen in waders, grabbing rods, stools and their netted catch but walking slowly back up through the wet sand to where they had their cars and vans.

"Go on lads." Came the collective shout from all the rowing lads.

"What the hell is going on?" I said, as Howard slapped me on the shoulder.

"They are illegal fishermen. They are poaching salmon. It's not permitted."

"Why are they all leaving now though, together?" I asked, quite bewildered.

"Well, if you look over there," Howard said, pointing to a big, blackened sandstone house on the quayside of Berwick's old town.

"That's the Customs House and you will see over there by the bridge, two blue vans with their orange lights flashing on their roofs, as they are just about to come over the river, and then to the carpark They have come to *catch* these poachers, red handed."

"But you can see them coming a bloody mile away." I said, turning to the others behind me who were, all either cheering the poachers on, the Customs Officers on, or me for asking an obvious and stupid question.

"That's why the poachers aren't in a rush. By the time the Customs Officers get down to the car park, they will have either stashed all their gear and salmon, or driven off home. It happens all the time and I don't think anyone has been caught in the past ten years, but still they come. I think it's considered a sport, on both sides."

Just as Howard had said, by the time the orange flashing lights appeared over in the car park, there wasn't a fisherman to be seen.

As the cheering and laughter subsided, a calm settled on us all. At the same time a brooding Jas arrived. He looked dour and taciturn after his day with the potters. His companions followed, first Liz, looking a little unhappy and then a slim and extremely pretty brunette.

"Ah, Jas, you are just in time to buy the next round," Howard shouted, reaching past me to slap him on his shoulder, and guide him towards the bar. "I will have a whisky and soda, if you please."

Jas flinched at being caught to buy the next round, and scowled unhappily, but he called the barman to his side and ordered drinks for everyone. Liz was speaking with her friend, but I couldn't hear. The noise from the others obscured their conversation.

"How would you know... How was it possible for me to know.... He seemed so nice at first....I had to stop him ... It was on my legs when I went to the bathroom."

77

They were facing away from me too, so I only caught a glimpse of what was being said.

Her friend had moved to my side of the veranda when the drinks arrived. Liz had left her, to collect two glasses of wine from the barman. The friend looked at me and smiled. She was about my age and dressed in a straight, sleeveless denim dress that fitted perfectly. When Liz gave her a glass, they laughed and leaned against one another familiarly, but without touching. She seemed to project an aura that was both attractive yet devilish at the same time. I moved closer, pretending to be interested in the conversation the men were having about scuba diving. Her voice was deep and sonorous; the hairs on my arms tingle in response to it, but more than that, my eyes were drawn to her perfect loveliness. I looked at her, a stranger, and every other breath strained to leave my chest.

A voice in my heart said, *yes, yes.*

"Ah, so you fancy her do you?" Jas observed, sidling in and handing me a pint whilst following the direction of my gaze. "You think she is beautiful, huh? Her name is Carmen."

"You met her today?"

"Oh, yes! Carmen's a potter and is half French and half Scottish," he replied, in a stage whisper so loud that I feared she might hear.

"You want to meet her?"

"Meet her?"

"If you want it, I will speak to her. You want her to be your friend?"

"What?"

"Carmen and I are friends and she will be your friend as well, I would think. Maybe you will become such good friends that you will have lots of sex together and have a lot of enjoyment."

Jas was actually rubbing his hand up and down his pint glass, in a provocative and yet creepy sort of way, whilst showing me his beautiful white teeth and curled lips of his smile. I had to grab his arm to stop him from approaching her, there, in the group of her friends.

"No! Stop! For Christ's sake, keep your voice down, Jas. If I want to speak to her, I'll do it myself."

"Oh, I understand," he said, looking abashed. "It is what you white guys call, courting."

"No! Courting is…. Never mind what courting is!"

"Oh good! I never mind about that stuff Peter, I am an Indian, and we Indians, we don't worry about courting. We go straight to the humping and bumping. Oh yes!"

He was holding an imaginary woman in his hands, along with his pint and was thrusting his hips forward, smiling all the while. A strange and sickly smile, with his eyes half closed.

"Will you stop that!" I snapped, looking up to see if Liz and Carmen were watching him.

"Okay, Peter, my man," he sighed, slowing his rhythmical thrusts until they stopped all together. "But, I can still introduce you to her, if you want."

"No! Thank you, I'll deal with my own introductions."

At that, I walked off in the opposite direction to lean against the veranda bannister further up, and watched the river swell as the tide came in. The sun was low and it was getting colder. The air was fresh and smelt of the sea.

I turned around, at that moment, and there she was again. Just inches away, both her and Liz, now talking to Howard.

I so wanted to tell Carmen that I liked her, and yet I hadn't even met her. But I did - I liked everything about her. I had liked her French-Scottish accent, and the way she pushed her hair back slowly as she spoke to Liz, I liked the easy, gentle way she touched her arm. She turned to look at me again and smiled and I melted at the way she held my eyes until the moment it stopped being comfortable, and then I smiled back softly and she never looked away.

Liz caught sight of our smiles and taking Carmen by her elbow, guided her over to where I stood, still leaning awkwardly against the railing. Howard joined the others as they walked towards me. As they stopped next to me, I tried to speak, to find some words, as I gazed into the amazing blaze of her hazel brown eyes.

"Peter, hello," Liz smiled and was about to introduce her friend. "This is…"

"Carmen, yes, I know." I interrupted her, not realising how rude that sounded.

"So, have you met already?"

"No, not at all. Jas was telling me how he had met her today, with you, that was all." I said, fumbling with my, now empty beer glass.

I felt numb, but my heart was moving at a pace.

"I haven't seen you in Berwick before, have I?" she teased.

"No, I guess not."

"So you are a friend of Jas'?"

"Well, I gave him a lift and he and Rick have sort of ended up staying at my place for a while."

"Peter is painting with my uncle, George." Liz added, which helped explain better, my awkward responses to Carmen's questions.

"Its a beautiful place," I remarked quietly, looking at her, but dreaming of something else.

"If you get a chance, you should drive up into the Cheviot Hills and then further north towards Edinburgh, where I come from." She said, making sure I heard that she wasn't a local woman.

"You have a gorgeous accent. Do I detect a French as well as an Edinburgh accent? Do you go to France often?"

She lapsed into silence, turning her head to scan up the river.

"Do you miss your home?"

"My home?"

"Yes, I mean where you come from. Don't you feel homesick?"

"Well, at the moment no. I've only been up here for a while and have left very little back on the South coast. Everything is so beautiful up here." I stopped, to catch my breath, and looked down into those dark hazel eyes, narrowed through soft brown lashes.

"Sorry, I'm going on a bit."

"No, no, please go on. I'm interested. You came here alone then?"

"Yes, I had the chance to paint water colours with Liz's amazing uncle for a summer exhibition and…"

"You know," she said slowly, "I like you,Peter."

81

She stared that hot fire into me. I felt myself reddening slightly, not from embarrassment, but from shame, that she'd said so easily the very words, *I like you,* that I couldn't let myself say to her.

"You do?" I asked, trying to make the question sound more casual than it was. I watched her lips close in a pouting smile.

"Yes, you're a good listener. That's dangerous, because it's so hard to resist. Being listened to is the second best thing in the world.

"What's the first thing?"

"Every artist should know that. The best thing is creativity."

"Oh, is it?" I asked, laughing nervously. "Really, most people would say, sex?"

She blushed and so did I.

"No, sex is a joy, but the best thing is to be truly creative. Just like painting a picture or moulding a sculpture. That's why I get such a rush."

I laughed again.

"And what about love? A lot of other people say that love is the best thing in the world." I asked.

I never got the chance to find out what Carmen's answer was as Liz, who had been distracted by Jas for a while, had suddenly come back into the conversation.

"What *are* you two talking about? *Sex,* already. For goodness sake, you've only just met."

She took hold of Carmen, by the elbow and as she turned away, gave me a wink and a knowing smile.

"Come on Carmen, you can go and see Peter's picture frames later on."

I was suddenly left standing on the veranda feeling the chill of the evening breeze, cooling my burning cheeks.

I felt good, really good and smiling, walked back into the club to find the others and get another pint.

Chapter 9

George and I had set up our easels, just a little way up from TweedMouth. It had started out as a grey morning, although not too cold, to sit out and sketch, but by midday the dark clouds, which had painted their sombre moods on the sky all morning, gathered from over the sea and seemed to press upon the tops of the tallest trees on either side of the river. The air was suddenly heavy with the scent of rain.

83

George pointed to the clouds and suggested that perhaps we ought to call it a day and pack up.

The first few drops of rain fell as we ran. In minutes the drops were a heavy fall and by the time we reached the Land Rover it was almost a cascade.

We sat inside and watched the rain on the river as it drifted and curled in sheets on the water. We watched the progress of the river as the tide ebbed, with its steep banks and the wide open plain beyond.

"Are we crazy?" I shouted, in exasperation.

"It's not funny!" George retorted, looking wet and miserable.

We sat and listened to the drumming of the rain on the roof of the vehicle and watched the darkness of the river.

George raised his eyes to squint at the racing clouds.

"If you don't mind Peter," he said to me. "I'm swimming in my clothes, and I will have to squeeze the water out of my old bones before I go into my house. I think it's time to go."

I stared straight ahead at the river, then glanced up at the black tumble of clouds.

"Yep, I agree. It's not going to stop. I'll take you home."

The rain did stop, but only just by the time I was pulling up outside Crab Cottage. There was a white, soft top Mini parked outside, in the spot that I had always previously used. I didn't think too much of it as I assumed it was perhaps a visitor to one of the neighbours or maybe even a beach walker, who had parked up for a while, but it was in *my* parking space.

When I reached the front door, I expected it to be at least shut, if not locked, but when I reached down to put the key in the lock, to my surprise the door was slightly ajar.

Pushing it slowly open, I tiptoed down the hall.

Sitting, quietly in the kitchen, was the familiar figure that was Jas. I sighed with relief.

"Why don't you shut the front door properly Jas? I thought we had a trespasser or been broken into."

His nut-brown skin was smooth and taut and his thick black hair was growing longer, as was his, once well trimmed beard. He was wearing a cotton kurgan, something I had never seen him wear before. I remembered them from my time in India. He turned with his usual smile. His thirty years sat lightly on his taller-than-average frame. He was a handsome man, and a great part of his beauty derived from his vitality and natural grace that supported his engaging presence. It was no wonder many women found him so attractive, but as he smiled at me and his eyes narrowed, my thoughts turned suddenly sour.

He suddenly spoke with a deep resonant voice.

"I have a gift for you Peter," he said, bringing up a blue and white clay pot.

"I made this for you in our pottery class, although I did have a little help from Liz and Carmen." He said, his voice changing to a more gentle and quieter note.

"It's to put your pencils in, maybe."

"Wow, great," I said, trying to sound thankful, as I took it in my hands.

"Gosh, a bit heavy and thick isn't it?"

The look I was given made me change my tone.

"But that's amazing, as it's your first attempt Jas, and anyway, it will be great for my - pencils."

Placing it carefully on the table, I turned it round to inspect the glaze, which was also rather thick.

"So, Carmen helped you make it, did she?"

"Well, she taught me to centre the clay and showed me how to use the right pressure to get the shape and everything. It's quite intimate, with a gorgeous young woman, wrapping herself around you while she helps you knead the clay. Guiding your hands with her own." He said quietly, gazing up at me.

I was suddenly feeling a little jealous and Jas knew it, as he slowly talked through his experience and demonstrated the intimacy, with his hands.

When he'd finished, he fell silent, waiting. I let him wait, but I knew he was only trying to provoke me. He no doubt thought I was weighing it all up, trying to make up my mind how to respond. In fact, although I was annoyed, I was only thinking about how to avoid an issue.

I smiled.

"I'll put the kettle on."

He smiled back.

Later on that evening when Rick arrived back and we had eaten, I suggested we walk over to the George Hotel for a beer.

"Why not drive over?" Rick asked complainingly. "It's probably going to rain again and…"

"No way, mate," I interrupted him looking out of the window at the thick, clouded sky.

As I did, I noticed the Mini was still there too.

"Whose is the Mini by the way?" I said turning to the other two.

"Search me, no idea. Probably the neighbour's car." Rick replied, not really caring.

Jas quickly avoided my gaze, for some reason, and equally as quickly, walked out to collect his coat that was hanging on the hook behind the door. Rick and I did the same and we all left together for the long walk over the bridge. As we passed the Mini, I looked at the number plate, trying to memorise the letters and numbers. I remembered the first two letters, an E and an N and the first two numbers, 64, but the rest I somehow forgot quite quickly.

The place was full with the usual crowd. They were all sitting in the busy, noisy, beery atmospheric lounge bar. The hotel served, what many regarded, as Berwick's best salmon dishes, in a town where all the restaurants vied for the honour. Despite that distinction, the hotel was relatively large but unknown. Its name did appear in the guidebooks and there was always an advert in the local newspaper. It was a local's place, and it was full most evenings. The meals were cheap and the decor was a functional minimum.

"Wherever you go in this town everyone serves bloody salmon and most of it is caught illegally." Howard was saying, a little too loudly we thought.

He was the only one eating while the rest sat around drinking their liquid dinners.

"You two coming to play tennis tomorrow?" he said, with his mouth full. "I'll take you both on again if you want."

The rest of the rowing lads laughed.

"Yes," I answered, slowly but steadily. "It was something I was going to ask you about. We'll come over in the morning, but only if the weather holds out."

"I will look forward to metering out more punishment."

We didn't finish the conversation as Trevor had suddenly appeared, forcing his way through the crowd with his elbows, brandishing a piece of paper and waving it in the air.

"You'll never believe it!" He exclaimed, thrusting a two page letter into my hands. I raised my eyebrows in great surprise. It wasn't just a letter, it was a declaration of peace - from the Russian Embassy in London and had lots of embossed gold crests and shields and even a red, wax seal at the bottom.

Trevor wasn't just happy, he was ecstatic. You couldn't imagine how pleased he was and how amazed the whole of the group was. Howard immediately stopped eating, and the rest stopped drinking.

Now that *was* amazing.

It wasn't a long letter, but it was very impressive with the gold headings and crest. The letter was from the Russian Ambassador himself. It was a Dear Sir letter. It was indeed, albeit tongue in cheek, a declaration of peace.

Trevor, tearing it back out of my hands, and in front of the whole bar, read it allowed, to almost total silence.

"For *fuck's sake!*" Jas hissed. "Not the fucking story about Berwick being at war with Russia - again."

Trevor garbled through the letter, speaking so quickly, and with his Berwick accent, that I couldn't make out a single clear syllable. His eyes were staring from his head. The effect was exaggerated by the size and shape of them through the thick lenses of his glasses, and his massive smile raising his cheekbones.

"What?" Howard said, putting down his knife and fork.

"It's fantastic," Trevor repeated, several times. "I actually got a letter. I actually got a reply. I was right. You see."

Trevor danced around us waving the letter over his head like a little boy with a new toy.

I asked him to repeat what he had read, but a little slower this time. Trevor did speak again, in exactly the same too-rapid, hyper-energetic manner, staring into my eyes as if he expected a monstrous kiss on his forehead or something. I was just as steadfast in returning the stare. I had been sitting, quietly watching this crazy man, but inside I was so pleased for him.

"He said that Russia has officially signed a peace treaty with Berwick-upon-Tweed," Les, one of the rowers, translated for me, in his thick Border accent. "Now he'll just go around telling everybody. Peace be upon him." He sighed, with a smile.

"Was there anything else?" I asked, mystified as I had already gathered that, but Trevor had gone on forever.

"He said that it was all due to his determination and research. He wants us to believe in him. Believe that he *is* someone."

Trevor laughed. It had been so rare to see him laugh out loud that I found myself laughing in response. I looked over at Rick who grinned back. Jas was standing in a corner, his face was drawn tight to the high cheek bones and the pointed chin, covered with his thick, black beard. His eyes, even in the bar's half light, were the polished dark bronze of a church cross. I knew though that his smile would reappear as soon as Liz arrived.

By the time she arrived, and with Carmen, Trevor had had several pints and was happy at being, very much the centre of attention and, for the moment, someone of importance and an accepted member of the gang of rowers.

"He's drunk. He got a letter from the Russian Embassy," I explained, as the couple drew near. I was shouting above the din. "He's very happy too, as you can see."

A roar went up from the crowd surrounding Trevor as they lifted him up above their heads, just missing the lamps over the bar.

I glanced at Carmen, her face was radiant as she watched the spectacle. She was beautiful, with her long, thick hair, styled to match the elegant cut of her long cotton dress.

It was a happy scene. Without Trevor's tenacity there wouldn't have been those historical findings. Without that hope, there would have been no reason to send his letter. Without his dream there wouldn't have been a reply and this declaration of peace.

The singing started and the group staggered towards the exit and the street. I watched Rick and Angus, who had become good friends, clasp arms and join the entourage. Moving through the door, they romped and rolled on the rhythm, their singing, drunken heads swaying like a field of golden barley weaving back and forth.

As the group disappeared and the noise subsided, I put down my glass and stepped out into the street and the cold night air, as a hand pulled at my arm. Carmen stood beside me. Her lovely, pale face was trapped in a fearful frown. I could smell her perfume as she was so close to me.

"Peter, can you get me a taxi?"

Worry pushed her voice almost to a whine.

It was my night to be the white knight. I looked into her large hazel eyes, and resisted the impulse to make a joke or a flirtatious remark. She was afraid. Whatever had scared her still possessed her eyes. She was looking at me, but she was still staring at the fear.

"Oh, I'm sorry," she suddenly started sobbing. "I'm just being silly, but it was the way he was grabbing at me."

"Who?"

"I didn't even say hello to you in there. How are you? I haven't seen you for ages."

Her lilting French and Scottish accent gave a fluttering music to her speech that pleased my ear. I tried to smile at her as the street lights streamed across her eyes.

"I'm fine. What's the problem and who's been *grabbing* at you?"

"I need someone to keep him away. Liz isn't always around and she is often with the others, leaving me by myself. Can you do it? Can you keep him away?"

"Who are you talking about?" I asked, becoming more concerned, as her voice was breaking again and she was on the verge of tears.

"Jas!"

"I trust you, Peter. I'll pay for the taxi, I'm not asking for anything else, if you will just be here with me until it comes. Will you do that?"

I heard the warning, I usually do, when something we can imagine is stalking us, and set to pounce. Of course I would help her, irrespective of her beauty and my romantic thoughts!

I smiled again, and hailed a passing taxi to stop.

"Sure, don't worry. I'll be there."

She came closer and gave me a kiss on the cheek. She got into the taxi. As she closed the door, she turned once more to smile at me.

"You'll be there ? Promise?"

"Yeah," I laughed. "I promise." The taxi pulled away and I watched it go.

"You bastard, Jas. What have you been doing?" I said to myself as I walked down the hill towards the bridge and home, aimlessly thinking about Carmen and what Jas might have done or tried to do. Whatever it was, I was going to find out.

Chapter 10

The following morning the weather had changed again and the wind, which had woken me at dawn, was streaming dark clouds across the grey sky. Struggling out of bed, I pulled the duvet back into position and tried to find some tennis looking clothes. The windows rattled as the North wind battered them relentlessly, but at least it wasn't raining.

I checked the front ones to make sure they were shut tight. One wouldn't close properly and leaked when it rained, another had a crack in the pane.

"One of these days, these damn windows will fall out or get blown in." I muttered to myself, forcing the handles down hard, before I went for a shower.

Looking out to check the sky, I noticed the white Mini had gone. We hadn't seen anyone get into or out of it. It had sat there, almost all week, and had never seemed to have been moved.

Well, it had gone now, so at least I could park my own vehicle in front of the cottage again.

Jas hadn't come back the night before and Rick was still curled up under his duvet and was not looking at all like he was ready to play tennis.

"Come on Rick. We have a tennis match to win, in half an hour." I shouted out, slamming the bathroom door shut.

I heard his muffled curse from under it.

The tennis match played out as it had before. Howard had successfully beaten us again, but at least it was a doubles match as Liz had decided to join in, teaming up with Howard, of course. Although Rick and I were both worn out, we did enjoy the games and certainly had needed the exercise. We were invited to drive up to a small hostelry on the Jedburgh Road where Liz's mother owned the pub, the Red Lion. It sat proudly on the top of a hill crest, with a view of the Cheviot Hills, she had told us.

Rick and I drove up separately to Howard, who was giving Liz a lift there, as she was going to stay overnight with her mother.

A short, but twisty drive from Howard's mansion, found us pulling into a small car park outside a red sandstone, slate roofed building, in what seemed the middle of nowhere. The four of us met outside the door, which had a low lintel and a notice pinned to it reminding us to *"Duck on entry!"*

Rick didn't see it until it was too late.

We made our way along the long corridor that connected the two bars, with Rick still complaining and rubbing madly at a developing lump on his forehead. A lady was sitting in the half light behind the counter in the back bar looking rather solemn. She scowled at Rick and I. There was a small hesitation as all three men looked at her, while Liz threw her arms around her mother's neck and gave her a big kiss.

Rick and I stood quietly, by the window as if we had been asked an impolite or embarrassing question, but when the old woman's eyes lit up at seeing her daughter and old friend Howard, I felt my heart stutter and we all laughed and relaxed.

We were the only ones there, standing in the middle of this little old Border's pub. The clock was ticking loudly on a far wall somewhere in the gloom. It was clean and fashionably bohemian, just like Liz, who no doubt had gained the same passion for the style from her mother.

She told us that local men from Berwick, mixed with farmers, fishermen and labourers from the area, often came for the well kept beer and her excellent home cooked salmon. She finally added that few tourists ever ventured in though. The elderly lady looked directly at Rick and I, as she made the last point. I liked the place, and I was glad that Liz had invited us up for lunch and of course, to meet her mother.

"Nice to meet you," Liz's mother said eventually, with a thin lipped smile and pulling at her apron.

"Where's that nice Indian fellow you brought here the other night Liz?" She enquired, hunching up her shoulders like a little girl would who had asked a naughty question and turning her head to get Liz's response.

Rick and I looked at each other instinctively. Liz caught the look and blushed. Howard was too busy assessing what was on the menu to have noticed or cared.

Liz didn't answer but instead grabbed a hold of the menu from Howard and read out what was available. Changing the focus and avoiding the question worked, as we eagerly chose from the sparse list of dishes, mainly salmon ones, having recognised just how hungry us tennis players were.

We worked our way through a big healthy lunch and apple pie dessert, and had moved on to our second coffee, so by the time we had finished eating it was early evening and a couple of farm workers had arrived for their first pints of the Red Lion's finest. Rick had sat at my left, with his back in a corner space, and facing the others. I could see the bar and Liz's mother. Her ageing face was handsome. Although she was probably in her sixties, she was physically fit but heavily set, with thick greying hair and the same shaped eyes as her daughter's, although her's, were set deep into the shelter of a high brow. She had a smiler's mouth and dimples just like Liz's. I watched her laugh easily, and it was a good, warm laugh. Liz loved her dearly and it was obvious to see why.

Before we had realised it, the sun had set and the racing clouds could no longer be seen. Rick and I had had a pint and decided to get home. Staying and having another would have no doubt led to more which would have been dangerously out of order and illegal, well for me driving anyway. We left Howard, with another pint being poured for him, and Liz who was staying overnight with her mother, sitting on a high stool in nook next to the smokey fire that they had just lit.

We rushed to the Land Rover, as it was cold and windy outside in the car park, perched on the hill alongside the pub. Howard's blue Mercedes was parked close by and an old farmer's jeep sat under some trees. Pulling out of the car park, Rick noticed another car though, with its side lights on.

He took a closer, second look as he seemed to recognise it.

"Hey, Peter, isn't that the white Mini that was parked outside our cottage?" He asked, straining to see through the window of the Land Rover and across the car park.

"Well, it's a soft top and it's white!" I mused, trying to look up and down the road as a car sped by.

"Must have just arrived. There's only one person in it. A guy, I think, sitting in the driving seat." He said, as we pulled out across the road to head home.

Howard didn't stay much longer and had said his good night's to all in the pub, before leaving and climbing into his car. He set off at his usual speed, with gravel and dust thrown up from his rear wheels as they spun.

For a while he hadn't noticed the headlights that had started following him. They had appeared shortly after he had left the pub, but were initially some way behind. Now they were up close and on full beam. He adjusted his mirror to avoid the glare, cursing the driver behind.

The car behind suddenly tried to over overtake him as a corner was coming up. Suddenly, it was alongside him as he braked for the corner.

"What the fuck!" he shouted."Hey, Watch out!" He mouthed at the driver. He couldn't see who it was in the dark, but his mouthing had at least alerted the driver, who swerved just in time to avoid hitting him. Howard was outraged at the sheer impertinence and stupidity of the other driver.

After the near miss he adjusted his mirror back and glared at the car behind, snarling a growl of insults. The car behind was being driven like a getaway car, slewing left and right, apparently trying to overtake. Howard was having none of it as he put his foot down, powering the Mercedes away, but there was an angry, bullying pugnacity in the driver's attitude. He rushed to within centimetres of Howard's rear, sounding his horn, then trying to nudge him out of the way. Howard moved a little to the left, in order to let him pass, but he drew alongside him again, pacing it for a time. Howard threw more insults, especially when he realised it was just a bloody Mini.

"This guy's a nut-case!" He muttered to himself, as a bead of sweat formed on his brow.

"For Christ's sake, stop this!" He shouted as the Mini accelerated again, lurching left and right.

"He's going to kill me!" He said, swallowing hard with fear. He hurled another pithy curse, but the driver only became more enraged. With the Mini hurtling along at top speed on the wrong side of the road and side by side with the Mercedes, the driver turned his head to snarl at Howard, who suddenly thought he recognised him. His mouth was wide open, and his teeth were bared. His eyes were huge and their blackness streaked with rage.

"Ahhhh!" Howard shrieked, stretching out his arms, forcing his body back into his seat.

It was too late. He turned quickly. His arms stiffened at the wheel, and he hit the brakes hard. There was skating then sliding, that seemed to take forever. Then there was the thump and crash as he slammed into a wall that had suddenly appeared on his left. Howard was thrown forward into the exploding airbag.

Shattered glass and chrome fragments rattled on the road like thin metallic applause in the sudden silence that followed the impact. Howard had hit his head on the side window as the car had twisted with the impact. With blood flowing from a cut above his eye, he swung open the driver's door and fell out, otherwise unhurt.

"Jesus, Bloody hell!" He said, his breathing heavy. "What was that all about and who the hell *was* he?" He shouted to himself.

The Mini was nowhere to be seen as Howard climbed back into his seat, shaking and scared. It wasn't long before he saw the blue flashing lights of a car, winding its way up the hill towards him.

He closed his eyes with relief and sighed, although his relief was short-lived as a police car pulled up in front of him and two burley men got out, slowly.

"Have we been having a wee drink sir?" Said the sullen Police Officer, now standing with one hand on top of the damaged Mercedes while the other hand was pulling out his notebook.

Rick asked me to drop him off in town on the way back. He was going to meet up with Angus, so I realised I would be having a quiet night in.

The cottage was dark when I parked up. As I got out of the Land Rover, I could hear the waves crashing onto the shore as I pushed open the front door. Jas wasn't in either, so I guessed I would certainly be having an evening to myself.

It was a couple of hours later, when there was a knock on the front door. I had just lit a fire and cursed as I wasn't expecting anyone and really had been looking forward to just watching the TV.

I opened the door and the cold rushed in, but I was so taken aback as standing there, with a handbag over one shoulder, was Carmen. She had a book in her other hand. Her long dark hair, falling in gentle curls that framed her face, trembled as she did. In the light, her pale skin stretched so flawlessly over the soft curves of her heart-shaped face, that for a moment, in the soft street light, she was a gorgeous Madonna.

I jumped with pleasant surprise as did my heart and I shamelessly kissed her on her cheek as I ushered her inside and out of the cold.

"Is it okay for me to just come over? I'm staying with Lisa, so down here for a couple of days."

"Of course," I agreed, waving her into the lounge.

"So wonderful to see you."

"Yes, me too!" Carmen added, rushing along the hall and out of the cold wind and into the warmth of the room.

"It's so cold out there tonight."

"You know the thing I like so much about you," I mused,"is your gorgeous French-Scottish accent."

"Is that the only thing?" She said as I closed the door, shutting us in the tiny lounge.

I blushed at my stupid point.

"Sorry, that was a rather dumb thing to say," I remarked.

"Tonight, I thought I would bring you a book I found, on old paintings of Berwick."

She whispered it and winked at me, the start of a smile tugging at the corners of her mouth.

"You may not be the first man that has commented on my accent, but you might be the first one that I haven't been annoyed by it," she said quietly. "Do you think I shouldn't have come then, as I hadn't been given an invitation."

"Not at all, I mean it's wonderful that you have come all this way, just to lend me a book!" I said, rather enthusiastically.

"Come and make yourself comfortable. I've just lit a fire and it won't take long to warm the place up. The other two are out so it's only me I'm afraid."

"Oh, that's fine by me. It's the right place and time for me, if you understand what I mean, and I will certainly make myself comfortable, by the fire, with you."

"It's funny you say that. I feel a bit like that myself. Within a few minutes of meeting you, I had an incredibly strong feeling that I would get on with you."

101

"Do you get on with Berwick as well?" She asked, but continued before I could answer.

"I knew that I would be at home here, when I came from France to Arran and then to Edinburgh, and now maybe everything is falling into place."

"Are you going to stay forever?"

"There is no such thing as forever," she answered in her slow deliberate way. "I don't know why you use the word."

"You know what I mean."

"Oui, Oui. Well, I'll stay till I get what I want. And then, maybe, I'll go somewhere else."

"What do you mean - *until you get what you want,* Carmen?"

She frowned in concentration, and shifted her gaze to stare directly into my eyes. It was an expression that I had seen before, and it seemed to say, *if you have to ask the question, you have no right to the answer.*

"I want everything." She replied with a faint, wry smile.

"Do you want to find love?" I asked, smiling.

"Yes, I think I do, but just a little bit at the moment. That's one of the reasons I came to see you. I like you and also respect you. I could never respect a man who didn't have a good sense to be at least a little bit capable of finding love too. Is that what you are looking for also, Peter?"

She stood up, and I rose with her. By the fire light her brown eyes were jewels of shining desire. Her lips widened in a half smile that was mine - a moment that was mine alone - and my heart began to hope and plead.

She was very still. She reached out with one hand to touch me. The hand rested on my hardening member, and then pressed with regular, gentle pressures. It was a tender,

102

reassuring gesture one might use to calm a frightened animal. She was staring into my eyes, but I wanted to know if she was asking me something or telling me something. She breathed deeply, quickly. Her brown eyes now looked almost black in the shadowed room.

She rested her face against my chest. I put my arms around her shoulders.

We kissed. Our lips made thoughts, somehow, without words: the kind of thoughts that feelings have. Our tongues writhed and slithered in their caves of pleasure. Lovers tongues. Lips slid across the kiss, and I submerged her in love, surrendering and submerging in love myself.

I lifted her in my arms and carried her into my bedroom. We shed our clothes onto the cold floor, and she led me across the room to my bed. We lay close, but not touching. In the low lit darkness her skin was on fire. I pressed my lips against the heat and licked the flames. She took my body into hers, and every moment was an incantation. Our breathing was like chanting as we explored the ravines of pleasure. We moved in a world of velvet cloaked tenderness, our backs convulsed in quivering heat. I was hers. She was mine. My body was her chariot and she drove it into the sun. Her body was my river and I became the sea. The final moan that drove our lips together in our ecstasy that flooded our souls with bliss.

The still and softly breathing silence that submerged us afterwards, was emptied of need, and want, and hunger and everything except the pure, exquisiteness of love.

"Oh, *shit!*"

"What?"

"Oh, Jesus, they're *back*!"

A twitch of panic and irritation creased my forehead with frown.

The front door had been slammed shut and I heard voices in the hall. Rick and Angus had both come back to the cottage.

Chapter 11

A few days later, I was returning to the cottage in the evening, having spent the afternoon with George and as I pulled up, a beautiful memory flashed into my mind. I smiled as I thought of Carmen. Although I hadn't seen her or heard from her since our interrupted evening of passion, she made me smile every time I had thought of her since. I climbed out of the Land Rover, slamming the door, and entered the cottage.

"Evening gents," I said, still smiling as I threw my coat over the chair and set my painting gear down in the corner.

I gave Rick a pat on the back, who ignored me, and made my way towards the fire. He was reading an article and was bent over, with his glasses resting on his head, in their usual position when he was concentrating on the small print.

"Special curry tonight." Jas suddenly exclaimed, rubbing his hands together and staring at me as he stuck his head round the lounge door.

"What's that look for?" I asked, feeling suspicious about how spicy he was intending to make it. He had done this before and on purpose it seemed, knowing that neither Rick nor I could endure the pain that his powerfully strong curries always provided.

"We've been invited to a party," Rick muttered without any real reason, not raising his eyes from the article.

"Up in Edinburgh. At Carmen's place. Some big expensive house under the Forth Bridge evidently."

He didn't seem too bothered, but I was and I was surprised too, as my heart missed a beat.

I wasn't sure if I was happy or not. Why hadn't Carmen asked me, directly? How come Rick was telling me this, I thought.

I was about to ask him, when Jas came back into the room, wearing only his sweat stained cotton vest that smelt of coriander, garlic and a hint of ginger. I could hear something frying in a pan of bubbling oil in the kitchen and wondered what on earth he was cooking.

A strange emotion haunted his face.

As he came closer, he turned to face me, and his eyes met mine. For a moment, those black eyes of his were directed straight at me. I didn't know why, but I felt uncomfortable. Strangely and suddenly, his mood changed and his lips curled into a smile although his eyes remained narrowed and focused on me.

"Liz invited us. All of us, on behalf of Carmen," he said slowly and deliberately. "Wasn't that nice of Carmen, Peter?"

I could feel anger and confusion both starting to bubble up inside me at the same time, when Jas suddenly became so pleased and excited at the thought of the party, that he exploded with a whooping cheer. He leapt in the air and danced a few pumps of a hip-thrusting sexy dance before the smell of burning oil arrested his dancing as he ran back quickly into the kitchen.

On the day of the party, I drove Jas, Rick and myself up to Edinburgh along the A1.

The coastal route with its magnificent North Sea views and breathtaking countryside was a joy and we were all now looking forward to a good weekend, in a great city and away from Berwick. The plan was to stay in a small, inexpensive Bed and Breakfast. Jas has phoned Liz to confirm that we were coming along with our arrival time.

I so wanted the chance to have a heart-to-heart with Carmen, that I could hardly contain myself and wanted to get to her house as soon as possible.

For days, after *that* night, I tried not to get too attached to her in my thoughts. I had found the joy of love and wanted to have more. I had sat alone on those many lonely and quiet evenings and remembered every word and every touch and every emotion. I had sipped a drink in a silence so profound that I could hear the sound of her breathing. The memory of the seductive, sensual movements of her body, had made me yearn for more and yet I was still confused.

Why had she not invited me personally? Why did it have to come through Liz and even worse via Jas?

I so wanted to talk to her, but in private and not really at a party and especially not at her party. The chances would be slim if not near impossible, as she would be hosting all her friends and probably wouldn't have too much time for me.

I sighed, breathing slowly and forcing calm into the little whirlwind that my mood was making out of my mind. I glanced out of the window as we passed a cove. It was windy and the tide was high. I saw the dashing waves below and the horizon in the distance, and suddenly felt much better. I smiled to myself as we drove on towards Edinburgh.

"The hotel!" Rick exclaimed, sliding his glasses down over his eyes.

"The B&B!" Jas corrected him, as I pulled up in a space just outside a four storey, sad looking building with a B&B sign, that badly needed repainting.

We checked in, showered, changed and we were ready within the hour.

When we drove off from the "Waverley B&B" to meet Liz and Carmen, I felt positive and hopeful for the first time in days. I began to think that I might have thrown off the dark mood that had settled on me after my night with Carmen. I had painted well with George, found some new places to explore and had walked the beaches along the coast.

Perhaps the world of possibilities was going to open up for me after all.

The house was on the South side of the river, in Queensferry. It was a T shaped red sandstone building with a slate roof and huge windows, each with Juliet balconies. The views from the North side of the house, looked directly onto the river and there was a wide stream running next to it that led to a small marina. I pulled off the road and into an expansive, gravelled drive and parked up. The open vista across the river was glorious and even the rust red magnificence of the Forth Bridge just added to the joy I felt at being there. The sun was setting behind us, which made the distant mountains and the bridge glow a deep crimson. Liz came out to greet us.

It was a postcard setting indeed, that inspired me to want to come back and paint here. The house had character and flair and as we entered the main room, I saw that it was a small masterpiece of light and clever, private spaces and it was so beautifully decorated. Walking into the dark, richly textured lounge, as the sun was setting, I paused and blinked until my eyes found Carmen with a group of friends. She and two other young women were sitting with Howard and another man.

"Hope we aren't too late," I said, shaking hands all round, including Carmen's. She smiled shyly at me and I smiled back.

"No, I think *we're* all *early*," Howard joked, his voice booming out across the room.

Carmen's two girl friends laughed hysterically. Their names were Lisa and Christine. They were aspiring pottery makers and they were all giggly and gushed up with arty words that weren't far off panic.

I sat down in a vacant chair opposite Carmen. She was wearing a thin, larva-red silk blouse beneath a black silk jacket, and a skirt. Her long thick dark brown hair blowing gently in the breeze, from the open patio doors.

The two friends were pretty, maybe in their early twenties, with long hair, both in pony tails. Their hands fretted with each other's, clasping and unclasping their fingers, as if they were turning clay

Howard was, surprisingly, in his usual tweed suit as if he were going to an appointment of some significance rather than a party.

More guests were arriving as Carmen served us some drinks.

"I'm starving," Lisa said happily. Her voice was light and confident with a soft west coast accent. She dragged Christine up and they disappeared. They both appeared strangely nervous, especially Lisa.

Carmen sat down briefly and squeezed my hand. It was an important party for her, bringing all her new found friends together for the first time. She was excited and wanted the party to go well.

"So pleased you have come," she whispered in her gorgeous French-Scottish accent and smiling, trying not to let anyone see her holding my hand. "I will try and introduce you to everyone. You've already met Lisa and Christine. They actually live down near Berwick. I'm surprised you haven't seen them with Liz at their pottery classes. Lisa has been acting rather strangely of late. Christine thinks that she might be pregnant, god forbid."

She was obviously still a little embarrassed about our relationship, and the possibility of her friend being pregnant didn't make things any easier I guessed.

The music got louder and the beer and wine flowed freely. Out on one of the balconies, drugs were being smoked quite openly, but the atmosphere was lively and everyone was enjoying themselves.

At midnight's horizon, when the clouds had cleared, the great milky wheel of stars had risen over the river, and the silver yellow light of a full moon settled on the water, glistening the tinsel crested tide.

It was a warm, still and perfectly clear night. The patio of the house was crowded, but I had managed to stake out a clear space a little distance apart from a group of young couples. They were stoned, most of them on grass and hash. Dance music thumped from the black speakers of the portable music system. Sitting uneasily on fold up chairs, they swayed and clapped in time, called out to one another over the music, and laughed often. So much so that no one heard the scream that pierced the air that night.

Chapter 12

Whilst Rick had spent most of the evening trying and sadly failing to chat up any of the young women around him, Jas had been trying to avoid Liz and instead had been seeking Lisa, but had had to wait to make his move as she and Christine seemed inseparable.

They were both a little drunk when Jas saw his chance, as Christine disappeared behind a bathroom door, locked it and immediately threw up.

Jas filled a couple of glasses and arrived just as Lisa was leaning against the door listening to Christine being sick. She felt sick too, but for another reason.

"A toast!" Jas exclaimed, raising the two glasses and clinking them, before handing one to Lisa. "To the freedom ...to love! *Salut!*"

He drank half the long glass, let out a loud, wide mouthed sigh of pleasure, and then drank the rest.

Lisa didn't take a sip from her glass, but held it close to her stomach.

Jas stood there dark and brooding. His gaze was dour and taciturn. Lisa flinched under his gaze and scowled unhappily, but with a smile and the promise of some time together to talk, he took her by the arm and lead her out to the side of the house and over the lush lawns to a line of spruce trees that swayed and rustled in the night air.

Jas guided her carefully, but firmly towards the boat house that nestled between the trees on a side stream that filtered into the main river. He had checked it out before and knew that there was a small wooden rowing boat tied up there.

Lifting the latch and kicking open the door he switched on a light. The dim light from the low wattage bulb barely lit their faces as he grabbed some oars, mannered her down the wooden deck and invited her to sit in the boat.

"I thought, as it was a lovely evening, and the stars were out and the moon full, we would go for a little row up the river."

"I think I'm pregnant, Jas," Lisa suddenly whispered, "and it's yours!" She exclaimed, taking a step into the back as Jas held onto the rope to steady it, her voice becoming a little bolder.

Jas untied the knot and taking the oars stepped in and sat down, facing her

"I had heard the rumour," he said, staring deep into her eyes, "but how could I know it to be true. How was it possible for me to know that you took no precautions? I'll tell you. At the start of our relationship, you were so eager to get your knickers off. I thought that was a sign, maybe I was a little bit too *good* at it for you?"

He rammed the oars into each rowlock and started to pull on them, moving the boat quickly out into the darkness.

"You ripped my dress off! I had to fight with you to save my clothes. And later when I had to go to the bathroom to wash myself out, as you refused to wear a condom, I came back to find you with a piece of rope, wanting to tie me up, and ready to do it again. I couldn't believe it!"

"Let's face it," Jas said quietly, "the crazy ones will always know how to find you and give you what you deserve, Lisa."

"What are you saying?" She said, trembling.

She was alone with a crazy one indeed, in a small rowing boat in the middle of a stream, being rowed steadily towards the fast flowing tidal River Forth.

Jas suddenly let go of the oars, letting them rest against the sides as the boat slowed and turned, dragged by the current. He leant forward and stared at her, his full beard majestic that covered his hard and hungry jaw. His black eyes were huge, within the caverns ridged by his brows. There was such madness and longing in them and he was at once fearsome and murderous.

He moved towards her, rocking the small vessel from side to side and smiling absently and she heard the little gasps of his breathing.

For a moment she was lost in his vision that swarmed and screeched in his eyes. She almost understood it, the smile of his, driven insane by the will that forced it to shine. He was communicating it to her - that he wanted her to know that she was going to die.

She could sense it and almost feel it, that terrible intimacy of a merciless painful death.

The vision shimmered as he grabbed at a natant oar, yanking it from its rowlock and raised the blade level with his shoulders and then, with a single, short angry cry, struck her hard, swinging it across his body to strike her head. Screaming, as she was hurled into the dark water, she surfaced, but only for a while as Jas pushed the semi conscious body back, deep into the water. The moment lasted less than a minute and then drifted away with the fading night shadows on the rippling water. He watched her body sink and her floating arms disappear. Then he turned, and tottered slowly backwards and sat in the back of the boat, still holding the oar.

In the bubble and chatter of the group on the patio, I checked on Carmen who had just walked out of the house with a group of men. Her eyes were wide and she pursed her lips in a wonderful smile as she caught sight of me. Reassured, I climbed out of my wicker garden chair and went to greet her. Actually, I wanted to steal her away from all the men that surrounded her. I stood beside her, watching the gentle rise and fall of her chest and the abstract gestures she was making with her hands as she engaged easily with a couple of the guys by her side.

I thought about leaving her to talk, but decided against it because I wanted her to talk with *me*, be with *me* - to ask herself what I'd been thinking and what I had been doing during the party in her house. To give myself an excuse to be with her, I picked up an empty glass and wandered towards her, waving it and suggesting that perhaps she needed a top up.

"You want to get me drunk?"she asked.

"No," I laughed, "but you'd be a lot better off getting another drink with me. More comfortable, anyway. My company must be better, surely."

She frowned, puzzled by my intervention, but was reassured.

"Are you coming?"

"Yes, I'm coming," she whispered, wagging the glass I had given her from side to side.

I looked at her. I stared into the sepia labyrinth of her hazel brown eyes and I wondered if she was going to play a part in my life, and if so, one of happiness or betrayal.

She reached out and put a hand on my arm. The grip was firm, but her hand was shaking. I wrapped my other arm around her waist. I felt the scent filled seconds expand around us. We were together, both of us, held together and once again we were about to set the web of our connection trembling.

"Relax. We are together," I said, calmly and lovingly."Now let's get that drink and you can tell me what you want from me tonight."

Howard and Rick were swaying dangerously near to the edge of the patio and urinating over the low wall, drunk and giggling, goading each other like small boys, as to who could piss the highest.

Suddenly, a man stepped angrily out from the darkness at their side, knocking the urinating pair, and sent them crashing over the wall. Their glasses fell from their free hands and Rick wet all down his trouser leg. The glasses smashed on the floor. Rick stood looking at his wet trousers as Howard snatched at the arm of the man who had shouldered them and held him in a firm but merciful submission hold. He gripped the man's arm in a hammerlock, behind his back. At the same time he twisted the collar of the man's shirt to choke off a little air. The anger or clumsiness that had possessed the man from the darkness subsided, and he surrendered passively.

Rick stepped forward as he recognised him. A second later, Howard also recognised who he had in an arm lock.

"Jas, what the fuck are you doing?" He said with a slur.

"Where the hell have you suddenly appeared from?"

"Probably *fucking* someone down by the river no doubt." Rick added, looking back down on the grass, trying to find his broken glass.

"But what's the fucking hurry and why are your shirt sleeves wet?" Howard said, realising that the arm he was still holding was soaking wet.

"Back off Howard. I was just having a piss like you, except I was pissing in the river not on the patio, shit head. Let go of my fucking arm will you. Dick head."

"You're the dick head. What's with knocking us over? What's the rush, man?"

"Mind your business. You think you are so fucking great, so amazing and all the women just adore you? Well you are a..."

"Hey buddy, just calm down," Rick suddenly said, interrupting him and raising his head, seemingly reconnecting with the world again. "Where did all that shit come from, man?"

Rick tried to look at Jas' face, but he had turned away and was already marching towards the house. Howard slapped Rick on the back and announced that he would go and get a fresh beer for them both and headed to the house following Jas. Rick just swayed a little more before falling onto a wicker sun lounger on the patio, his glasses as twisted as his drunken smile, and closed his eyes.

Leaning against a door frame and trying to hear what Carmen was saying, with the loud music and the general buzz of the party in the next room, was proving difficult. I was about to shout into her ear that we should move outside, when Jas, storming past us, knocked my elbow, spilling beer over me. Howard, wasn't far behind, but he was rather drunk and sidled past with pursed lips and an angry stare that seemed to be aimed at Jas, just in front of him.

I was about to say something as I wiped the beer off the front of my trousers. Carmen thought it was funny and laughed, but although the wet patch was in a rather awkward and potentially embarrassing place, the fact that Jas had caused it, stopped me from laughing too.

We were all rather drunk by the time Howard staggered past us again, this time with Liz on his arm, heading for the patio.

Carmen and I decided it was time to attempt the stairs to her room.

The side lamp was on and with the curtains closed, the bed looked very inviting, as did Carmen.

The last beer, just before I fell on the bed, was my final one. The urge to close my eyes and surrender to the alcohol swept over me in almost irresistible, immersible waves.

"Don't try to get up." Carmen said, kneeling beside me and loosening my clothes.

I laughed, because standing was the last thing on my mind. In the laugh I felt the dizziness, dimly through the haze of the beer.

"What's going on, Carmen?" I asked, hearing my voice warble and slur as I spoke. The distorted speech and my creaking fumbles were all I could manage.

"What are you doing? What am I doing?"

"Did you think I would let you just fall asleep here, when I need you so much?"

"And I need you too, Carmen, but I.."

"I know," she said, staring into my eyes with such intensity that it cut through my drunken haze like sunrise piercing the morning's mist.

She smiled, and the smile was wicked and sexy. I was suddenly sober and I saw our chance to find ourselves again. That was the power behind her intense stare and gorgeous smile. She was ready to do anything and everything.

"I know what we need," she whispered, laying on me, raising herself with her arms to arch above me. I tried to sit up to speak to her, but she just laughed quietly, undoing my belt, and it was wonderful to see and hear her laugh that I took those bright, round syllables of happiness into myself

118

like food, like drink, like a drug. Despite my drunken state, I knew with perfect understanding that the greatest treasure and pleasure I would ever know was in her laugh; to make Carmen laugh, and feel the laughter and kisses from her lips against my face, my skin.

"I have told you before,"she said,"that a good man is as strong as the right woman needs him to be."

Then she grasped my hardness, and I closed my eyes. Hours later I opened them to find Carmen sleeping close beside me.

Chapter 13

Carmen had been in the shower and was dressing, when there was a knock on the door and I heard her invite the person in.

It was Liz, who told her that we ought to come down stairs. I dressed and we both walked quickly along the landing and down the staircase to the lounge. A crowd of party goers from the previous night had gathered there and as we walked in, we could hear the pitiable crying of a woman sitting on the sofa.

Liz and Howard were standing close to her as we pushed our way through the silent group to join her.

Two policemen were standing over her. It was Christine.

"What's happening?" Carmen demanded.

"There's been a wee incident, a drowning," one police constable replied, turning in the direction of Christine. "A young woman's body was found by a boy walking his dog this morning. It was lodged in some tree roots in the water here, and there is a rowing boat tied to the landing further up the stream."

"What makes you think it has anything to do with us?" Carmen demanded.

Christine, still with tears streaming down her face, looked up at Carmen.

"Lisa disappeared last night. I just thought she had slept somewhere else as she didn't come back to the room and she wasn't in bed this morning. The description of her clothes......" her voice trailed off as she cried even more.

"We should never have gotten so drunk and then she wouldn't have fallen into the river." She continued, wailing through her words.

The policeman drew his brows together in a fierce frown, and stared angrily at her.

"Oh! and another thing," the policeman said. "Her handbag was in the boat but there was no purse, credit cards or money. She had been robbed, as well."

"This is not the first time that Lisa has got herself into a mess. I could have stopped it."

"I...." Christine began as she let the tears flow again, but she couldn't hold the stare, and she looked down at the at her white knuckles in her lap. There was a kind of rage in her. "She had got herself pregnant, and that was because she was drunk then."

There was a sharp intake of breath from both the policemen and the crowd in the room.

I looked across the sea of faces trying to see who was there. Howard looked pale and shocked. Rick just looked terrible.

Several of us stepped away and some paced the room. The room became more crowded as others arrived.The gathered group became intertwined in their disbelief and shock, their movements slow and without purpose. And like most people everywhere, they were reluctant to interfere, ask questions or offer information, especially with such a terrible situation.

I reached out and put a compassionate hand on Carmen's shoulder to calm her.

Just then a new burst of activity entered the house, followed by raised voices.

Several of us stepped back, determined to make room for the arrival of several more policemen. They surrounded everyone in the room. The group flinched and recoiled in horror. They were all affected by the sheer horror of what had happened. As the police told us all to remain in the room, we were all stricken with pity for Lisa, and for some reason, shame passed between us, burning our eyes.

The shock that had paralysed us escaped in a collective gasp, as we rushed forward to stop Christine falling on the floor as she fainted. Howard wrapped a blanket around her shoulders and held her up as others lifted her back onto the sofa.

A senior police officer took charge of the scene and ordered us all to remain in the room.

Suddenly and for no reason, I looked round to see where Jas was. He couldn't have left last night as there was no way of getting back into central Edinburgh, but I had no idea where he'd slept nor where he was now. All I knew was that I couldn't see him in the room.

The policeman asked each of us what and how much alcohol we had been drinking and whether there had been any drugs used. The answers were short and mainly inaudible.

They sat Christine in a circle of police women, who offered her comfort, as they questioned her. Carmen and I were separated and asked the same questions as everyone else. The officers glared at us all suspiciously, but encouraged us with pats on the back, to be honest and open. The younger officers were more forceful in their coaxing. Then, some twenty minutes after being interviewed, we were allowed to leave and we all gradually drifted outside to exchange our thoughts as well as what we had said, seen or heard.

Rick and I would have left then, but Carmen asked us to stay and anyway, we still hadn't found Jas. Nobody else seemed to know where he was, not that many seemed to care either way, except Liz. She had wondered where he had got too, as she was sure she had seen him earlier that morning, heading for the front door, not long after she had made herself some tea.

Carmen handed me a glass of water, without me asking for it. I sipped the cold liquid gratefully and wondered where Jas could possibly be.

When Jas had woken that morning, the sun was just coming up, and his distress was great. He cursed himself, but found no solace in his own chastisement. He could see himself that he wanted to refuse the thought of what he had done the night before. He scrambled out from where he had been hiding all night, in the cupboard under the staircase, and grabbed the bottle he still had, with trembling hands. Just as the first drops touched his furred tongue, he heard

123

the sound of footsteps coming along the landing above. Rum spilled over his bearded chin, and ran from his gaping mouth. He dropped the bottle and tried to scramble back into the cupboard on his hands and knees, but he saw that the front door was open and decided to make a run for it instead. He just made it before the footsteps started down the stairs. He pulled the door too as he left without looking back and ran out towards the road. As he ran, he looked up at the mighty iron bridge that towered above him. He had no idea where he was running to, but he knew he needed to escape from the house, pull himself together and decide his next move.

The mood in the house remained sombre. I sat with Carmen. Someone turned a radio on in a room up stairs, and a sad love song wailed along the landing and down the stairs. A woman was crying somewhere. People milled around outside in a circle, looking tormented.

I walked into the kitchen to make some tea for us. Others had gathered there too, making toast and cups of coffee, trying to bring some normality back into the house.

I thought about what we had heard and tried to recall events, anything that would help us understand what might have happened the night before. I thought about who was there when the police arrived, and indeed who wasn't. It was quiet, in those dark, thinking moments; quiet enough to hear my heart beating whilst watching the tears fall from the sorrowed face of many guests.

One question kept my mind confused and buzzing.

Where had Jas been and where was he now?

One day became two days, and one week became two weeks. From the time of the party, the police had supposedly been investigating the death of Lisa.

A month later we did hear that the forensics had determined that she had hit her head on a branch near where she had moored the boat herself and as she had been drunk, had knocked herself out and drowned.

The reason for her empty purse was never determined, although the police seemed to think it was the boy who discovered the body, who had taken the items from the boat.

I didn't see Carmen at all during that month, but I did receive a series of strange and bizarre messages from various people with news of her. I was sitting alone at the table in my cottage one morning, painting, when shouting roused me from my work with a flurry of swear words and angry tones. There was rage and terror in it. I put down my brush. The front door was thrown open and shafts of golden morning stabbed through the gap to the lounge where I sat. More shouts and screams followed.

It was Rick and Jas.

Jas burst into the lounge, swaying from side to side, scanning the room with his large, dolorous eyes. I stood up, too surprised to speak or move. Rick was just behind him, hurling abuse and questions.

"So, where the fuck were you that night, Jas?" Rick screamed at him, trying to grab his arm and pull him back. He succeeded in spinning him round, and stood close to his chest with his hands firmly holding onto Jas' shoulders.

"And tell Peter about Liz and Carmen," he said, his teeth bared and his face red with anger.

Jas took a crumpled, white envelope from the pocket of his jacket and held it up for me to see.

"A message?" I managed to ask.

Rick's strong arms and chest were well muscled and easily held Jas still until he stopped ranting. His long black hair and beard were thick and he looked tired.

I stared at the envelope and felt a hand on my arm, and almost jumped. Rick drew my attention back with a stern look.

"We are lucky that you have taken us in and put us up, Peter. You didn't have to let us stay. The least we can do is not hide things from you."

"I didn't hide this, Rick. What the hell are you saying? What do you want from me? I was going to give him the fucking message."

"Carmen wrote you a letter, and gave it to Jas to give to you, ages ago. I only found out when I spoke to Liz this week."

"Give it here." I demanded, holding out my hand.

The envelope had been sealed originally but had been torn open. I assumed, by Jas.

"Why is it open Jas? Did you open my letter?"

"Of course he did damn well." Rick bellowed into Jas' face.

"Too many fucking secrets, too many coincidences and too many unanswered questions. Like where was he when Lisa died and how the fuck did he get back here and why leave and not wait for us?" Rick was almost purple with rage. Beads of sweat had formed on his brow and as his muscled

126

arms flexed, and his hands shook, his anger exploded out from deep within him.

He moved even closer to Jas, shouting more questions as I opened the ripped and crumpled envelope and took out the message.

It was indeed from Carmen.

My darling Peter,

I hope you are well. You have told me how much you love me. I think I feel the same even though we have only known each other for such a short time. I think you must be lonely by yourself and with the death of Lisa, like me, perhaps a little lost and much in need of comfort at this time.

Liz and I have grave reservations about the way the investigation is going about what happened. It seems that the police think it was an accident.

Liz told me she saw Jas leave early and both you and I couldn't find him the following morning.

We should have told the police perhaps, but I trust you have asked him since, and there was a perfectly reasonable and simple explanation.

I'm sorry we haven't spoken but it is still hard to forget what happened that night. Perhaps we can meet soon when I next come down to Berwick to see Liz.

God bless you and take care.

Lots of love.

Carmen xxx

Rick was standing by my left shoulder, as I read the note again, slowly.

"So you read this, did you Jas?" I said, staring coldly into his dark eyes.

"It's rude to read other people's mail, Jas."

"So, why did you?" I continued, looking back down at the page.

"And why, having read it, didn't you give it to me straight away?"

"Were the questions raised in it of concern to you? Do you have something to hide?"

"Yes, sure it's a bit rude but there's no harm done." Jas said, after a while.

He was looking directly into my eyes and into my soul. I could feel the hairs on the back of my neck stand up with the discomfort of his gaze.

"Very rude." I muttered, reading the letter over again.

Jas went to the open door of the cottage and paused there, staring at me reflectively with his black bushy bearded head cocked to one side. I put the letter down and looked up at him. I thought he wanted to say something. There was a little struggle of concentration in his brow-but then he seemed to change his mind.

He shrugged.

He smiled, what seemed more of a grimace than a smile.

"You've made your point. I'm going now."

He walked out, and I was alone with Rick, who sat down heavily on the sofa as the sounds of the sea swarmed around us: the waves crashing, seagulls squawking and the wind whistling through the fences.

We both knew something wasn't right, we knew somehow, deep down that evil and Jas were somehow wedded together, but nothing made sense and we had no proof of anything.

I was depressed and yet anxious, angry and yet fearful. I needed to get back to painting again and called George to arrange a day out with him, somewhere up the river.
I had phoned him and he suggested a quiet spot just west of Berwick on the south bank of the river, at Kelso. I told Rick that I would be going early as I was looking forward to visiting Kelso and finding a spot on the river banks, although I was sure that George would already have a place in mind.

The following morning I left early to meet George for our usual pre-painting breakfast. The High Street was already busy and the sun was shining. I took in deep breaths of the air, sea salt and seaweed, as I crossed the road and listened to the calls of the black headed gulls and oyster catchers.
It was a great drive up on a gorgeous morning and it didn't take long to find the place that George knew I would want to paint. The river swept round with amazing views and we soon settled down to paint. We worked quite urgently. George was single-minded and systematic in his pursuit of capturing the light perfectly. He painted with style and ease, but he was always very generous with his complements, believing in handing them out to me as I struggled to capture reflections off the water as the clouds came over and the light changed. We both knew the

troubles the darkening sky would bring. Yet there was happiness with every brush stroke George made, and an excitement in the easy smile that never seemed to leave his face. After a couple of hours of frantic work I put my waterproofs on and finished off, packed my things away. George had a plastic sheet that he erected over him and his easel. He wasn't going to let a few spots of rain stop him. It was only going to be a shower, he said, still smiling as I decided to sit it out in the Land Rover. I trudged off up the bank and along the road to where we had parked. I sat in the back as the rain got heavier and waited for George, thinking he would no doubt give up soon and come and join me. He didn't come.

Jas parked up in a clearing, down from the bridge in Kelso., and took out of the boot a wooden baseball bat. Rick had told him about the painting trip by the river. He had watched Peter striding up the bank and along to his Land Rover leaving George under his plastic sheet.
It was easy to quietly sneak up to him, from behind.
George didn't see Jas coming from behind his screen. It was raining harder and the wind rustled the leaves above and the plastic sheet over George. He pulled back the sheet and struck him over the head with the bat, flinging him to the ground. George raised his arms in feeble pleading, but further blows hammered on his face and chest. It happened in seconds and there was no time for him to react.
What we call cowardice is often just another name for being taken by surprise, and courage is seldom any better than simply being well prepared.

The beating was swift, but savage. Blood streamed from George's head. He howled and screamed as Jas lifted him up. His arms were splayed out at right angles and his head lolled and fell back, a soft, wet flap of skin hanging from his cheek. His eyes were open, but he was barely conscious, staring backwards and upside down; scudded with fear and imbecile hope, as Jas dropped him into the fast flowing water of the Tweed.

Barely ten minutes had passed when the rain stopped so I decided to go and find George. I was just putting on my jacket, when I was interrupted by shouts and a scream.
I rushed out of the back and ran towards the sound. Not far away, I saw someone climbing into a car, a white Mini and was shocked to see that George was no longer where I had left him. His easel was lying on the grass and his paints and brushes scattered along the bank. I looked for the Mini but it had already driven off at high speed. I looked for George along the bank and then in the fast flowing water.
He wasn't there.
He had just disappeared.
A splinter of fear and panic pierced my heart when I realised that something terrible had just happened. Helpless, craven, ashamed, I hadn't stayed on the bank with him.
"I've got to do something…" I said lamely to myself.
My self assurance had melted through muscle and bone to settle in my knees. Each step was suddenly leaden and willed. It wasn't just his sudden disappearance that had shaken me. It was, instead, the dread that he had fallen in

the river or been pushed, or worse, especially as I had seen someone getting into the Mini.

The same Mini that had stood outside my cottage in Spittal? "What... what am I going to do?" I cried, still searching the river water for signs of his body. I stumbled stupidly along the bank, through bushes, ripping my fingernails and scratching my hands. The brambles tearing at the skin.

There was no sign of him and nobody else was around. I sat down heavily on the wet bank. My hands were shaking as I took out my mobile and phoned 999.

I sat and waited, but for me the sudden, bewildering disappearance, the sight of the overturned easel and brushes strewn across the grass and the thought of George floating away on the ripple of the river, was a turning point. A new understanding emerged from it.

I suddenly realised, with the death of Lisa and now this, that there could be a murderer in the midst of the people I knew here.

In the distance, I heard the wailing siren and saw the blue flashing light of a police car. I was about to become involved. Berwick wouldn't let me walk away from this and remain apart. I had to expect that she would drag me into the river of her rapture, and her rage.

Now I would have to step off the pavement and into this bloody scene, and put my body on the line.

And with the seed of that resolve, born with convulsion and portent, my dark involvement began.

The police arrived and quickly manhandled me into the back of the police car for questioning. It was obvious that I was indeed the primary suspect.

One of the policemen whispered to the other after joining him in the front of the car. I tried to hear what they were saying. They turned round and were suddenly making a joke and talking about trivial, unrelated things. Finally, one of them made a remark that tightened the skin on my skull and face with dread.

"So what have you done with the body," one of them said. "Threw it in the river, did yee." His Border accent thick and deep.

"Aren't you that wee boy from down south. Got friendly with our pal, Howard." The other one said.

They went on accusing me. They argued a little just to intimidate me. One of the policemen was more forceful. The other agreed at last, with the idea to take me to a quiet car park in Kelso, and then beat me until I confessed.

It was bizarre, sitting in the back seat of a bloody police car and listening to the threats and what would happen to make me confess. My stomach dropped and tightened on a curdling mix of nausea and rage. I hoped to hear a clue, some reference to a motive, but they never mentioned one.

"Listen!" I said at last, my voice and hands trembling. "This is monstrous. I've told you about the white Mini. If you know Howard, then ask him whether his incident involved the same white car. Isn't that a bit of a coincidence, officer?"

He smiled, and turned round in his seat and nodded.

"All right then mister Hanson. We will go and see Howard and see what he says, but you are going to the cells for the time being."

At that moment, more police cars arrived with the emergency services and the area was cordoned off and a river bank search started.

People were on their phones and donning white suits and wellingtons.

I nodded to the officer, saying nothing, but my silence prompted him to speak again.

"This doesn't mean you are not still a primary suspect." He said.

"By the way, young man. We found some coins on the bank, but no wallet anywhere."

"No, I understand that officer, but I didn't do anything to George, or steal his money."

He was staring at me intently, his hands still resting on the steering wheel.

Be careful, I thought. You're getting into a dangerous discussion with a police man who automatically thinks you are guilty. He's testing you. It's a test and the water's deep.

"Let me get this straight mister Ianson - you are still our prime suspect, and in saying that, we are taking you in. Anything you say now will be taken down a possibly used in evidence against you - laddie."

"You are saying that at the moment because I am here. *I* phoned the emergency services, remember. Why would I do that if I was guilty?" I said, pushing a canoe of thought out into the uncharted water of the idea.

"So you agree that the possibility of me being innocent is beginning to grow?"

He ignored me and started the car and with blue lights flashing, they drove me to a police station and escorted me firmly into the duty room.

I was being arrested.

The awfulness of it buzzed and swarmed in my whirring mind. Did they really suspect me? If not, were they really looking for someone else? If they thought I had nothing to do with it, what and who else were they looking for?

There were more questions This time by a small and officious inspector, followed by an identification procedure, my belonging and fingerprints taken.

I had to get a message out to ......someone, anyone. Who could help me? Who was willing and powerful enough to help me? Howard. With his contacts in Berwick and obviously it seemed, in the local police force, he would surely find out that I'd been arrested when the two Kelso policemen went to ask him about the white Mini. Assuming of course that they would go and interview him. I had to sit tight, say nothing.

They marched me down a prison cell corridor. The duty officer ordered me into a cell. He stood in the doorway to the lock-up, watching me with his fists on his hips. At one point he shouted at me to get my laces out of my shoes and remove my belt. He wasn't impressed when I pointed out that wellingtons don't have laces.

I saw the steel bars on the little window above and heard the solid door slammed shut behind me, and felt the creeping coldness numb my heart. Metal slammed against

135

metal. The keys jangled and turned in the lock. I sat on the wooden bench and stared at the floor with resentful fear.

Somewhere, deep inside me, a drum began to beat. It might have been my heart. I felt my body tense and clench as if it was a fist.

I was innocent, but the hatred for the person who had done this was like a thick and bitter taste in my mouth. I struggled to swallow it down.

Chapter 14

The local police station had only four small cells leading off the corridor. I spent the night huddled on the wooden bench seat with only my jacket to keep me warm, listening to a couple of drunks swearing at each other and the police, from two of the other cells. They fell silent, no doubt from the drink, about an hour after being locked up. I was woken on the hour, every hour with the sound of the metal spy hole cover being pulled back and a Scottish voice asking me if I was alright.

As dawn broke, the door suddenly opened and I was asked if I wanted any breakfast. I hadn't had time to sit up, let alone reply, before I was told what I was going to get.

Twenty minutes later I was served a half cup of cold sugarless tea, a cold sausage and two hard fried eggs and baked beans.

I asked to go to the toilet which was down the corridor and smelt of urine and shit. The urinal was full.

I remained in the cell for most of the morning, pacing back and forth, wringing my hands and hoping that somehow I would be given the chance to clear my name, get out of this nightmare and try and help find who had done this. I received another cup of cold tea at four in the afternoon. It was cold - again.

An hour later, the door was opened once more and I was led down the corridor to a small office. I saw three men - the arresting officer, a plain-clothes inspector with short grey hair, and Howard - sitting around a wooden desk.

"Howard!" I shouted. "Thank goodness you're here."

The two policemen exchanged neutral glances, but said nothing.

"What *are* you doing here?" Howard said straight away.

I was about to reply when the inspector leaned over to me. Taking that as his cue, the inspector coughed, and gestured towards Howard.

"This gentleman, mister Baxter, has confirmed that there *was* an incident involving himself and a white Mini, on the Coldstream road just recently, and our records indicate that to be the case as well, but the officers investigating the incident could not identify the driver and searches for the Mini, without any information concerning the registration number, have so far proved fruitless."

He rested his hands flat on the wooden desk, and his fingers rolled through once in a little Mexican wave.

"No way, inspector! You haven't found it even *now*. How many white, soft top Minis are there in the Borders? We had one parked outside my cottage for days." I said, without thinking about what I had just revealed.

I suddenly looked up at the inspector, who leant back in his car and folded his arms.

"We know about that and I was wondering when you were going to tell us." He sighed and then turned to the arresting officer, hunching his shoulders and raising the palm of his hand in a question.

"We didn't know whether mister Bellingham was alive or dead until this afternoon. We found his body, washed out to sea, beyond the mouth of the river, down in Berwick. The initial forensic information suggests that he was beaten unconscious with a blunt, wooden instrument and he either fell or he was thrown into the river. We think he was attacked from behind and probably didn't see his killer. We

138

also think he might have been robbed as there was no wallet or money in his pockets, but if you remember, we found some coins on the bank."

I stared at the inspector. A fever of fear was stinging my eyes, and the effort it took to sit upright in the chair was causing me to sweat and shiver.

"I'm going to be honest with you mister Ianson, although I believe your story, and we did find blood stains along the bank near where you saw the Mini, we still need to ensure that we know where you are at all times, as we might need you for further questioning in the future."

Half an hour later, I rode with Howard through the early summer countryside, with the evening sun shining and the passenger window open, breathing in the fresh air, on our way back to pick up my Land Rover, made me feel a little better. Howard glanced at me and asked if I was okay. I felt nauseous when I looked into Howard's eyes. I never said a word, except to say how grateful I was that he had come. I was crying, softly and silently, when he dropped me off on Kelso bridge.

When I got back to the cottage, I spent two hours in the bathroom, thinking, showering and clenching my teeth against the anguish. I looked in the mirror at my red eyes and saw George's face smiling at me. The last smile I would ever see. I tried to erase the picture that raced through my mind of him being attacked, just metres away from where I was sheltering in the safety of my vehicle.

Rick was there and was pleased to see me and especially as I had been released without any charges. He had heard through the Berwick grape vine about what had happened, about both George's disappearance and my arrest. Word hadn't really got across the fact that George had been found dead, under suspicious circumstances.

"Hey! How are you, buddy?" He enquired, quietly.

He placed a hand on my shoulder.

An unusual gesture for him.

"Let's go for a beer, Pete." He said, more of an instruction than an invitation, I thought.

"I'm not driving Rick and I'm exhausted and upset, but I could do with a *walk* and a beer."

Rick smiled and handed me my jacket.

"Where's Jas?" I asked, as Rick escorted me out of the front door, slamming it behind him.

"Haven't seen him today, at all. Why do ya ask?" He enquired as we strolled up towards the bridge to get into town.

"I always want to know where he damn well is?" I said, pulling up my collar, and scowling.

We arrived at the pub and were greeted by the rowing club guys. Liz was there and began to cry as soon as I walked in with Rick. I sat down next to her and wrapped an arm around her in the automatism of grief and shock. She didn't really look at me or acknowledge me. I patted her shoulder and rocked her from side to side but her sorrow-struck expression would have been the same if she were alone and wrapping her arms around herself.

"I don't know what to say Liz," I said. "I am so pissed off. The police weren't helpful. They wanted to blame me, but when they saw the blood on the grass and the tyre marks, they were sort of convinced it wasn't me."

"There are a lot of people in Berwick who believe you were responsible." She sobbed. "We've just heard, they found my uncle's body."

The crowd in the pub were looking at me. One started shouting abuse as he moved towards me.

What I could make out from the many people now shouting, was that they were simply wanting to attack me. Suddenly, a man appeared beside me and seized my jacket and began to punch me about the head and face. I had no idea why he'd attacked me - maybe he didn't understand that I wasn't responsible - but it didn't matter. The blows were struck and I was the reason. I covered myself with my hands and tried to wrench myself free. His hand was locked onto my jacket, and I couldn't shake him off, so I stepped in closer, crashed my fist into his head above his ears. His hand released me and he fell back, but others decided to punch me as well. The crowd at the bar opened out around me and I started punching at anyone around. That's when the rowing club boys started to lay in.

It was a bad situation. I knew sooner or later I would lose the energy and will to keep the drunken bar throng at bay, but then the determined group of eight rowers broke through the circle and punches started to fly freely until I had arms wrapped around me and I was dragged out of the writhing, lunatic hell that the bar had become.

Howard wiped the blood from my face with a handkerchief. My eye was swelling up quickly and blood was dripping from my nose and a cut on my lower lip.There was no pain.

We were out in the street.

"Ah, christ," I moaned "Ah fucking hell."

"You're okay now. I'll get on it," Howard said, quietly and with confidence. "We will help find out what happened and who did this. We will find … him. The cops are on our side, well mine actually, but I'll make sure Pete, don't worry."

I looked at the faces around me; faces struck with compassion and dread. In the eyes of some, I saw shame for what the locals had done to me, but in others I saw the fear that a second person they all knew, and loved, had been suddenly and violently, taken away. Murder hadn't been mentioned specifically, not even now, but the incident in the pub was making it quite clear that the crowd in there thought so, at least.

"Great that you are safe Peter," said Trevor, dabbing his mouth with a blood soaked tissue. "But it is worrying that we seem to have a murderer in our midst." He continued, as we watched the crowd leave the pub and hobble away up the street.

"I don't know what scares me more," Rick declared," the madness that seems to be surrounding us, or the fact that we don't know who it is that might have murdered two people."

Most of the crowd had now left the pub as the police arrived. They had finally been called.

At the same time, Carmen suddenly drove up with Liz, and stopped. She had been staying with Liz at her mother's pub, when she had heard about George Bellingham's death. Liz was still too upset about her uncle, and she looked pale and tired. Carmen got out of the car and came up close and I put my arm around her shoulder. She turned to face me, and I kissed her.

The taut bow of her lips dissolved on mine in concessions of flesh on flesh. There was such sad tenderness in it that, for a second or two, I floated free. Her kiss was pure and the gentle loveliness of it shocked me but my lower lip still hurt too much, and I pulled away.

"I'm sorry, I didn't….." I faltered.

"It's okay," she smiled, leaning away from me with her hands on my chest. "I know. I bet it hurts!"

The wind had gotten up and lashed her hair into her face, and she pushed it back with both hands, holding it there with her fingers fanned out across her forehead.

She was staring down at her feet.

"What the fuck is happening here?" She rasped, her lips drawn tightly over her teeth.

It was a question that I had no answer to.

"Howard dealt quickly with the police and so Rick and I weren't interviewed, let alone arrested, thank goodness. I don't think I could have coped with another round of local police *hospitality.*" She said.

Carmen drove Rick, Liz and I, back to the cottage where we found Jas who had just lit a fire. When we entered the lounge, the orange glow and radiant warmth were a joy.

143

Jas stood up when we entered and smiled at Liz, before seeing my bruised lip and black eye, and scowled.

"What the hell happened to you, Peter?" He said, appearing shocked, and held his arms out to me. I refrained from moving any closer, as did the others. No one wanted to explain what had happened and least of all, to Jas.

Rick had disappeared but returned with four shots of single malt whisky, so we took a glass each and sat down quietly and gazed into the flames while sipping the warm liquor.

The silence filled the room and could be cut with a knife. Nobody wanted to start a conversation, especially with Jas there, whose behaviour we all had concerns about since Carmen's party.

"Don't I get one then?" Jas finally asked, looking at us all with our glasses.

"Erm, sorry Jas," Rick murmured, "didn't think you would want one."

"Well, why not?" He enquired, staring at each of us in turn.

"Well, you haven't exactly gone through what Peter has, have you?" Liz spat the words out and glared back at Jas.

She started to cry again. There was a terrible anguish written in the rivulets of her tears. She swayed and sobbed in utter silence. Carmen opened her mouth as if to speak, and decided to close it again as she too dissolved into tears. I looked up at them both and with an effort of will, I clenched my jaws to white that set my body trembling. Carmen swept her hands over her face, and her crying ceased. She was very still. She reached out with one hand to touch me. Her hand rested on my thigh and squeezed. It was the tender, reassuring gesture I had become accustomed to from her.

Liz brushed at the knees of her jeans, picked up her bag, and stepped past us towards the door.

"Come on,"she said to Carmen. "Time we went home. I need to see my mum."

For a moment we looked at the two of them as they stood together. I felt tired and angry and confused. I watched Liz stand impatiently in the doorway. As Carmen stood and walked over to her, I did too and led them along the hall to the front door. I grew more sullen and resentful with every step.

"I'll see you tomorrow?" Carmen enquired. Their expressions told me that Jas was watching us and listening, as we spoke.

"It's fine. I'll call you tomorrow." I told her, hoping she wouldn't say anything else.

They quickly gathered themselves, and left me to close the door behind them and go back into the lounge.

"Well, what the fuck was that all about. Let's have a beer?"Jas said, rubbing his hands together.

Rick stopped me at the doorway, and gave me another glass of whisky. He stared into my eyes, with a - calm down look - and then helped me, with a firm hand, into a chair.

"What do you mean, Jas?"

"I'm talking about what's up with everyone. Stuff happens. They were crying their eyes out. Carmen - what was it all about?"

He glanced at Rick, who stood close by me, impatient and proactive. Rick looked back at Jas, his eyes puzzled and tired.

"Do we have to talk about this now?"

"No, we don't!" Rick answered before I could say anything.

"I'm not talking to you," he snarled, not looking at Rick, his eyes fixed on my face.

"You really are a bastard." I said, directing my angry response at Jas.

"You're overreacting, Peter."

"*I'm* over reacting!" I said, almost shouting.

"Shut up, Jas." Rick said, just as I stood up to confront him.

"Look, Jas. There are some terrible things going on. Lisa's death and then what happened up the river with George. How did anyone.... You know, how did anyone know we were up there? I only told Rick here and I'm sure he didn't have anything to do with it."

"I told you, Jas, where Pete was going with George." Rick said slowly and quietly, looking straight into Jas' eyes.

"Oh, so *you* knew as well did you? Well maybe you ought to have told the inspector that you knew. And while we were at it, I saw that white Mini again. It sped off when I reached the river bank. You remember the Mini, don't you Jas. It was like the one that sat outside here for ages and like the one Howard described that tried to run him off the road," I was shouting, as a pearl of sweat trickled from my temple across the fold wing of my cheek. "All too much of a coincidence perhaps, don't you think?" I stopped, realising I had maybe said too much.

"So what? I just don't think there's much any of us can do about it. Let the cops do their job and stop trying to suggest there is some sort of conspiracy going on." He snapped, a flash of hate and spite in the gleam of his clenched teeth.

"Who mentioned conspiracy, Jas?" Rick suddenly said, quizzically.

Jas suddenly looked unsettled and then stormed out of the room, to the kitchen and began to open the back door, but with the wind howling off the north sea, slammed it shut again and went to his room, slamming that door too.

Rick and I looked at each. He wasn't smiling, and I had the feeling that we both thought there was more to Jas' involvement than he was letting on. He drained his glass, examined its emptiness for a moment, and then placed it gently on the table.

"Let's get drunk, Peter !" He said at last, but my hand stayed his, preventing him from reaching for the bottle.

 "I can't, Rick. I have to get some sleep."

He smiled slowly, and slid his handout from under mine. Still staring into my eyes, he raised his hand, pointing with one finger. He poured another tot.

I had a fitful night. The wind rattled my bedroom windows and my head and face hurt. My mind raced, disturbed about the recent events, but the one thing I couldn't get out of mind was, the white Mini.

Chapter 15

On the following morning, when I finally got up, I walked slowly up the beach, and gave myself time and space to think. Carmen hadn't called me, and although I had left her messages to tell me where she was, she hadn't and I had no idea where she might be. I had woken that morning with a dream of her as my thoughts now drifted to her again as I struggled against the wind.

My conspicuousness was a strange sort of camouflage. Foreigners from down south were stared at in Berwick. But now, somehow the culture had decided to dispense with the casual, nonchalant glance. Because of what had happened to George, a well loved member of this community, the eye contact ranged from an ogling gaze to a gawping, goggle-eyed glare. There was malice in the look. The staring eyes that found and followed me the day before were not innocent or curious. I had been and would continue to be scrutinised intensely. It might have a benefit though, I thought, as I reached the end of the sandy spit. They would stare me into invisibility in the end, not wanting to be associated with me.

I turned around and walked back, but past the cottage and on up the wide mouth of the river, lengthening my stride as I neared the shipyards and the dock, and as I strode on I asked myself who would really have wanted to murder George and Lisa and why? It still nagged at me that Jas always seemed to crop up somehow in every incident.

It felt as if *I* was the only one keeping secrets, and no matter how thick my mind became with the thoughts of George's murder, of Lisa's suspicious death, of Howard's incident with the Mini and with Rick's near accidental suffocation, whilst diving in the harbour, I had never told anyone that Jas had always entered my mind, or that others had seen

149

him around at the same time, or just after one of these *incidents*, or conversely, he was never with the rest of us at the time when these terrible things had happened.

I had just reached the gates to the shipyard, passed several parked cars. There was a white Mini, but my mind wasn't really on any further investigations today. At the end of the yard, I hung a left and made my way along the Spittal road. I had needed the walk and had found some peace in doing so. As I rounded the next bend I heard the sound of a car horn and a voice calling my name.

"Hey! Peter!"

I turned to see Howard leaning from the driver's seat of his car. I walked over to greet him.

"I've just been to your place. You weren't there so I was on my way back home. Jump in and we'll grab a coffee and a bite for lunch."

"Thanks, Howard," I smiled. "I've been walking to try and clear my mind. I'm glad that we've met as there are some thoughts I think I should share with you." I said, as I closed the car door.

"The world is run by loads of evil men, ten times more stupid men, and one hundred times more cowards," Howard pronounced as he put his foot down and we pulled away at speed.

"The evil men have the power. The rich, politicians and religious fanatics are the ones that set the world on its course of greed and destruction. Sadly those decisions really count. The stupid men are those that enforce the rules of the evil men. The police are sadly part of that. They are

150

brave, but they are stupid, as is being shown now, unable to catch this "murderer" that we seem to have in our midst."

"And the cowards?" I asked, as we reached a junction.

"The many more cowards, are the bureaucrats and paper shufflers who allow the rule of the evil men, and look the other way. They are the sort of people in the pub that attacked you. They always defend themselves by saying that they are just following what they have been told, or just doing their job in society, and it's nothing personal, and if they don't do it - beat you to death, then someone else should and will."

He fell silent as we drove over the bridge before turning right into Berwick High Street to find somewhere to park. A few moments later we found a spot and stopped. He shook himself from his reverie and looked at me, his eyes gleaming in a gentle, affectionate smile.

"So that's my thoughts," he concluded. "The world is run by evil men, stupid men and cowards. The rest of us, billions, do pretty much what we are told."

"We have a murderer somewhere in this town and they might be closer than we think." He suddenly announced, looking down towards Berwick's fortressed, red sandstone walls.

He looked away and shifted the ground as he changed the subject. He was skilled at performing the trick and it always caught me off guard.

"That's what I wanted to talk to *you* about, Howard." I said. He frowned, and I had to look away from his penetrating gaze. It gave me a bizarre rush of pleasure to hear that he too was perhaps thinking the same. Still, I didn't want to

151

make accusations that I couldn't back up, even to myself. The play of conflicting emotions- suspicion and disbelief, facts but no proof - confused me. The confusion emerged as irritation, in my eyes and in my voice, as I told Howard all my thoughts.

We'd been sitting and talking in the car for half an hour. Finally, enough had been said and Howard and I stared at one another in the silence, I didn't speak. I didn't answer his question. *Do you think you know who the murderer is?*

Of course I had my own suspicions. I had been living amongst it all. I wanted to know everything, but I wasn't happy to play Howard's question-and-answer game either. I didn't have any proof, and suspicion without proof, would make me the same as the *"cowards"* that he had described.

"There are only two questions that need to be answered," he said finally, without looking at me as he gripped the steering wheel.

"Who *is* the killer and why would they want to kill *these* people?"

"And don't forget what happened to you and Rick either, Howard." I reminded him, as we both had decided, enough was enough - for now that was.

Liz called me while Howard and I were sitting in the front window of a little tea shop that nestled under the high walls that surrounded the fortified area of the town.

"Peter?"she asked tentatively, as if she wasn't sure that she was speaking to me. "I've got uncle George's collection of paintings here in front of me. Mum and I are at his house

152

and found them in his studio. The exhibition is due in a couple of weeks and we would like it to go ahead, but I don't know which paintings he was intending to exhibit," she stumbled through the words, trying not to cry. I could hear the sadness and concern in her voice. "Would you... do you think you could come over and help decide which ones?"

She stopped abruptly and obviously was waiting for an answer from me.

"Well of course I will," I said, not really sure which work he had intended to show. "I can certainly gather all the work that he was creating over the past couple of months, from the places he took me to."

I waited for her to reply. There was a long sobbing silence before she spoke again.

"The last painting he was working on, by the banks of the river in Kelso, with you, was unfinished and because of the rain, it is all smudged and the paint has run. I know it looks weird, but it was the last piece of art he painted before...."

"Do you want to put that in the exhibition?" I interrupted, quietly, wondering if it would really be a wise move.

"I don't know," she snivelled, "that's why I need you here."

"Okay, I'm coming. Howard and I are just having a coffee and lunch in Berwick. He will bring me over, if that's okay?"

"Thank you so much, Peter. I'm very grateful and I know George would want you to choose which paintings. He spoke very highly of you and your painting skills too. He often told me how much he enjoyed spending time and talking with you."

"I'll miss him too. See you soon." I said, ending the conversation abruptly, before turning my phone off and turning to Howard, who had been able to hear most of the conversation. We left the cafe and got back into Howard's car and drove off.

We spent the rest of the morning going through his work. There were plenty of beautiful water colours, but as I knew he wanted the exhibition to focus on the river Tweed and especially with regard to the places that he and I had sat for several hours, trying to capture its beauty and power, I chose fifteen paintings, gained Liz and her mother's approval and collated them ready to take them off for framing.

George was a popular person in the area and his house had always been a meeting place for musicians, writers as well as other artists. Liz had spent many days with him learning to make pottery with her mother, in the studio there. She had watched him magic the blank paper and canvases with all the colours and shapes of his passion.

To have lost him before the up and coming exhibition, had torn her heart in two. Her misery was ruining her beauty, and had already killed her piano pottery making and was in danger of smothering her life as well.

Howard, without her seeing, passed me a bottle of sleeping tablets that he had seen sitting in her open bag. We were both concerned now that she was perhaps thinking of taking an overdose.

154

That same morning, Rick had woken to the sound of the kitchen door closing. His head was a little sore from the night before and extra whisky he had drunk, once Peter had gone to bed.

He climbed out his bed and opened his curtains a little to see Peter striding up the beach. The need for coffee dragged him into the hall. The door to Jas' room was open, so he looked in. Jas wasn't there, but Rick spied on the top of the dresser, a thick, leather bound book. He hadn't seen it before and was intrigued. He opened it and saw that it was Jas' journal. He wondered why he had, perhaps stupidly, left it on the top, but was delighted to have an opportunity to sneak a look. It was filled with entries in his own handwriting. Knowing that he shouldn't, Rick turned through the pages and read his private thoughts. It wasn't a diary. There were no dates on any of the pages, and there were none of the day-to-day accounts of things done and people met. Instead, there were fragments. Some of them were culled from articles and newspaper headings, each one attributed to an incident of missing people or disappearances and annotated with his own comments and ideas. There were random writings that described what he had been thinking or feeling on a certain day. Other people were mentioned frequently, yet they were never identified as he or she, except once.

On one page there was a cryptic and disturbing reference to the name Lisa.

THE QUESTION: What will Lisa do now?

155

THE ANSWER: Lisa needs to go.

His heart began to beat faster as he read the words through several times. He didn't doubt that Jas was talking about the same woman - the pregnant Lisa that had died in the terrible accident at Carmen's party, the Lisa that Jas had spent a lot of time with. And it seemed from the strange couplet, that she knew something about him perhaps. Rick wondered what it meant, but the more he thought about it, the less he liked its possible meaning.

Rick examined the pages before and after the entry more carefully, but found nothing that might connect Jas to Lisa's "accident". On the second to last page of the journal, however, there was one passage that clearly referred to Liz.

She wants to tell me that she is in love with me. Why did I not let her? The night before had been amazing. She said that she liked my smile. I am glad she said that as I want her now, as well.

Beneath that entry he'd written the words:

I don't know what frightens me more, the power I have to crush her or the endless ability to watch her suffer.

Rick couldn't get the words out of his mind and standing there, at the dresser top, he snatched up a pen and copied out the words on a sheet of paper. With the stolen words folded secretly in his wallet, he closed the journal and replaced it exactly as he had found it.

He walked out of the room and decided to follow Peter along the beach to tell him what he had found. The warm sea breeze helped blow away his hangover. Looking right, along the beach he expected to see Peter at the end of the spit, instead he had obviously been that way and was now walking up the other way towards the wide outlet of the river. He decided to follow him.

On his left he passed the shipyards and the dock where there was a large space. Several cars were parked round the edge next to a pile of timber and some steel girders. Nothing grew there, and the whole area was dusty and run down. He decided to take a short cut between the parked cars so as to make up a little time and catch Peter up. As he worked his way in-between the cars, he glanced at one that for some reason had caught his eye. It was a white soft top Mini. It was parked alongside several other cars and covered in a thin film of dust. He knew it was like the one that had been parked outside the cottage in Spittal and was horrified to think that it might also be the one that Peter had seen, driving away at speed from the river bank at Kelso, after George's disappearance.

Had it been dumped there? It certainly hadn't been moved recently, he thought, wiping a finger through the dust on the bonnet.

Putting his hand over his brow to look through the side window, he peered inside, but saw nothing on the seats or the floor that would give him any clues as to whose car it was.

He read the number plate, NC66 and tried to memorise the combination of letters after that, but decided to try and catch Peter up and tell him at least the first part.

He checked his watch. He reckoned he was probably only a few minutes behind him, as he raced through the rest of the parked cars and up to the road. Looking both ways but not seeing Peter anywhere, cursed and then cursed again when he recognised Howard's big blue rebuilt Mercedes, disappearing up the road.

He guessed that he had picked Peter up. Fumbling in his pockets to find his mobile phone to call one of them, he realised that it might not be a very good idea.

Although he thought of ringing the police, he decided to wait and show Peter what he had found in the journal and in the dockyard, when he next saw him. Hopefully later on that evening.

Rick was making dinner when Peter arrived back.

He was later than Rick had expected, and looked tired.

"Hey there buddy," Rick said as he turned from the cooker, spatula in hand. "You look pretty worn out. Glad you are home though. I'm making dinner if you want some, but first, I'll pour you a beer as I need to show you something."

Rick showed Peter the words he had copied from Jas' journal. Peter didn't appear to be as shocked as Rick had expected, but both decided to keep it quiet for the time being, especially when Jas bounded through the front door, smiling broadly, as he always did.

Rick grabbed at the notes he had made and folded them quickly so he could hide them in his trouser pocket before Jas had time to see them.

158

Chapter 16

Rick and I discussed Jas' journal and the Mini again the next day, a week before George Bellingham's funeral.

"Do you remember the number plate on that white Mini that was parked outside of Crab Cottage?" Rick asked me.

"I can only remember the first two letters and the first two numbers, I'm afraid Rick."

What were they?"

"Why are you asking now?" I asked, suspiciously.

"Because, I saw a white Mini down in TweedMouth dock yard, covered in dust and sea salt. Looked like it had been there for some time."

"Well, I remember the first two letters were E and N and I think the number was 64, so a 1964 registration."

"Mmmmh, well a different car then," Rick sighed. "The registration I saw started with the letters NC followed by 66. I didn't get the rest."

"Strange coincidence though, Rick. The same car but two years younger." I said, wondering whether he had got it right.

"Maybe though, it was the same car, but with a false number plate. Perhaps the plates had been switched." Rick said, tilting his head on one side, questionably.

"You've been watching too many gangster movies, mate." I said, nudging his arm and smiling.

A week later, just before the funeral, everyone was starting to talk about their fond memories of George, whenever we met, and obviously we were all getting upset. Liz, with her family, along with Howard, were very involved with Jo matters surrounding the funeral and so we all tended to leave them alone to manage things. I hadn't spent any time looking after Carmen, who had come down to stay at Howard's mansion, to help support Liz and her mother.

Just after I had had the discussion with Rick about the Mini, I did find time, when Jas was out the following day, to look in his room. The journal wasn't where Rick had found it initially, on the top of the chest of drawers, and as the bedside cabinet was locked, I assumed it had probably been hidden away in there.

Although we both had our concerns and indeed fears, Rick suggested we get out of the way for a few days and asked if I would take him to Goathland to see his distant cousin at his farm. As it was the initial reason why he had been making the journey up to the North East of England in the first place, when I first picked him and Jas up, I agreed and said we should try and go soon and he agreed as he had already spoken to his cousin.

Sometimes, looking back, I deeply regretted that day, but then that seems to be my life!

Rick had made contact a few weeks before and with a short phone call to confirm our visit, we had decided to make the journey the following day. The farm we were heading for, was in the middle of the moors and it was a good job that I had the Land Rover as it turned out.

Rick didn't seem to be concerned that for only two people, we seemed to have several tonnes of cargo in the back. These weren't gifts from Canada, but from local shops or from Edinburgh, purchased and stored over the weeks since he had arrived. When we reached the single track roads, my old Land Rover began to sway on its exhausted springs like a tugboat in a storm tide. Creaks and groans and squeaks issued from all parts of the floor as we travelled across the narrowing roads. We were doing fine until we reached a precipitous fall on one side and a flock of moorland sheep on the other. I think my vertiginous hostility with which I now negotiated every curve, was

161

sufficient to relieve Rick of the need to sleep or even relax on this latter part of our journey.

During the last forty minutes of that perilous ride, we rose to the peak of a ridge before descending to the bottom of a beautiful valley. With a prayer of gratitude, and a new appreciation for the fragile gift of life we arrived and Rick left me sitting in the Land Rover, while he went to knock on the front door of his cousin's farm house.

He strode up to the entrance but before he could get there, his cousin sprang out through the arched porch, grabbed him, as if he were a giant bear, and they embraced with gusto. His cousin's smile rivalled that of Rick's. The family resemblance was quite strangely striking. It was a vast smile, using the whole face, as if it had been frozen in the middle of a belly laugh. When Rick turned to face me, besides his cousin, subjecting me to a double dose of the gigantic smile - the original, and its slightly grander genetic copy - the effect was so overwhelming that I found myself grinning helplessly in return.

I shook hands, and Rick and his cousin stared at each other. They had the same rounded face and strong nose. There was pride in both their faces, but his cousin was sad and tired, and worried. It took me a long time to realise that all farmers, everywhere, are just as tired, worried, proud, and sad:that the soil you turn and sheep you feed are all you really have, when you live with and work the earth.

"Come in, come in. I've been expecting you all morning." His cousin waved me to a place to his left. He kicked off his boots at the doorway, where a pair of green wellington boots had been discarded too, and sat down in a rather old and battered leather chair. It was a large room with a long oval oak table in the middle of it. The floor was surfaced with dark brown terracotta tiles. A square of carpet covered the tiles in our part of the room, near the huge range log burner. The walls had old paintings covering them. An open arch connected the room to a long passageway. A large picture-seat window overlooked the barns and the hills beyond.

It was a room of old austere splendour. There was little furniture except for the few chairs and the table and in the corner a deep, sage green velvet covered settee. His cousin looked very comfortable in that inornate simplicity, however, and certainly there seemed to be a hidden wealth of a rich old farmer.

"My cousin is a very successful man," Rick beamed, proudly, his arm around his cousin's shoulders. His cousin patted his pot-belly, his eyes glittered as he spoke.

"I've got a few things in the car for you! A few presents." He said, as he got up and we all followed and stepped out of the room to go back outside.

"Why, I'm doing alright, just about me lad." He said, with a hint of a Tyne side accent and we walked to the Land Rover, where Rick climbed into the back and started to unload the vast number of gifts he had brought. We took them back inside to be opened later.

His cousin was called Jack. A busy but not very worldly sheep farmer. His manner was quiet and his words were few. After all the initial greetings, he said he had some jobs to do, so Rick and I followed him out to his barn and into a dark corner near a rusting trough full of dirty looking

163

water. He lit a cigarette and I watched him startup his chain saw then drag a large log over to a tree stump, surrounded by wood chippings and sawdust. Without a second of hesitation, he raised the large chain saw and clicked it to life. It screamed like the whine of a jet engine. Jack looked at Rick, and a huge grin tore his mouth open. His teeth were clenched in a smile as he drove the saw into the wood. With four swift, ear splitting cuts, he had divided the log into nice sizable chunks, ready for his log burner.

I realised that this was going to be a long and perhaps arduous day so decided to leave them to their reunion and wandered back out of the barn, over to a dry stone wall and gazed across the distant moorland. It was quiet, apart from the bird song that was drowned out every time Jack's chain saw ripped up the peace and quiet.

The sound of my mobile buzzing in my pocket, suddenly jolted me away from the distant hazy horizon.

It was Howard.

"Yes," I answered, slowly but steadily, wondering whether it was going to be bad news.

"How are you?"

"I am well, thank you. I'm with Rick. I brought him to Goathland to meet up with his cousin and was just gazing out from his *humble* surroundings."

"Not so humble then, Peter?" Howard remarked.

"He actually owns a fair few hundred acres and a load of properties." He laughed, then carried on.

"Do you fancy having some fun?"

"Certainly, I do.I've had enough of crap things happening."

"I thought you might,"he said.

"Would you like me to rescue you from your miserable life by inviting you to a party at my place, a fancy dress party?"

"That's if you wouldn't find it too painful with what's happened. We all feel the same I think, so I thought we all needed something *uplifting*. After George's funeral, of course."

"Yes, thank you. That would be great." I said gleefully, my sudden loud voice startling a pair of starlings that had been pecking for grain over the wall. The birds flew up and flapped around my chest as I moved away.

Howard's tone suddenly changed though, and he sounded a little uncomfortable as he spoke.

"Peter, there's something else I want to say, before we.... talk about anything else," he began quietly. His next words drew my head up swiftly as he suddenly had my full attention.

"It's about Jas."

"Yes, go on," I murmured.

"Well, I thought about it a lot since the other day, what we talked about, and what you told me and I have a problem with it." He stopped for a while.

"I know, I'm not saying this very well, but all these instances where Jas has been there. They just don't feel right. No matter what this guy is up to, I don't want to be put in a position of being... well a policeman, but although I can't help feeling that he is very much involved with what's been happening, the phrase *helping police with their enquiries* is a euphemism for informing on someone and round here, it's sort of not done. I'm sorry, I know that Jas *might* have been involved somehow in their deaths. If you want to go after him, that's your business, and I'm happy to help you out in any way I can. But I don't want to be involved with the police myself as they sort of know me."

"Is there anything more?"

"No, That's .... That's..... pretty much it."

"Very well, Howard," I replied. My voice was impassive, but inside I was quite angry. "I totally understand your situation. I won't mention you or involve you any further.. Okay?"

"Yes, yes. Thanks Peter. I knew you would understand, and I will send you an invite to my fancy dress party tomorrow."

"Well, I'll be happy to come. I assume you will be inviting all *three* of us then?" I stammered, bewildered by his request not to be involved, but not daunted by it. I felt competent in dealing with the issues I had dealt with every day of my life. My mind was hot, my thoughts scattered and flapping like the birds I had startled with my voice. There had to be a solution to solving this, but if people around me, who I thought were close allies, were suddenly beginning to drift away, afraid of becoming involved, I was more than concerned that these *deaths might* just continue.

Who would be next? I suddenly thought, as a cold shiver ran up my spine.

Rick came up behind me and placed a hand on my shoulder. I jumped and turned as my body tensed.

"Mercy me, buddy." Rick said, a little startled by my response.

"Oh, sorry Rick. I was miles away. You surprised me." I felt the shiver run up my spine again.

166

"I was just talking to Howard. He's invited us to a party. To help us get over Lisa and George," I said, trying to smile and put a positive, upbeat spin on the request.

"Hey, man, that sounds great." Rick smiled back, recognising that I wasn't seeming to be over joyous.

"It's going to be a fancy dress party, so we had better get our thinking caps on." I replied, patting his chest.

"Is Jas invited too?" He asked, tentatively.

"Of course." I said, trying to sound both pleased and nonchalant, at the same time.

At seven o'clock, after a hearty evening meal of roast lamb, fresh garden vegetables and a glass of local ale, we decided to head back to Berwick. Cousin Jack had other ideas though, and insisted that we stay over, and having agreed, he proceeded to lay a wonderful selection of different cheeses out on the long oak table, along with a couple of bottles of port and enough oat biscuits to take us through the night.

That evening was good for me. There were a lot of words, there was a lot of friendship and family and I remembered, just about, that there was a lot of love that passed like whispered prayers as the talk and laughter crashed around me.

When the light on that long night became the dawn, and the sheep could be heard, demanding to be tended too, I was the first to stagger to the front door and let in the morning sunlight. Forcing my feet into my shoes, I walked across the farmyard and through a leafy grove, past the outhouses to a style over the dry stone wall.

None of us had made it to bed the night before, but instead, each had collapsed into various chairs and sofas, in the lounge, inebriated, but happy.

It had been good to watch and listen to Rick and his cousin, Jack, tell family stories, recounting memories of times past together, and with long gone other family members.

I heard Jack's somewhat shaky voice, cursing at his noisy sheep as he tried to get his two dogs to round them up.

The strong smell of the farm and the moorland gorse and heather first thing in the morning, forced me to close my eyes and embrace the new day with joy.

Our world is a magnificent place, I thought, keeping my eyes closed and opening my nostrils. Feeling the morning sun on my face and soaking up the pure delight that was the countryside, made me smile and realise how lucky I was to be alive. I realised I was standing near them with my eyes still closed. They had walked up behind me and I found myself eavesdropping in their conversation. Jack asked Rick if he had any money, if he could manage on the savings that he had and whether he was paying any rent. When Rick told him that I was letting him stay at the cottage for free, he asked if he was working or just living off the savings he had brought. Reassured that I hadn't been ripping them off,

I was nicely surprised when Jack thanked me for supporting his cousin and handed me some money...... to help pay for Rick's stay.

I hadn't been expecting it, but I wasn't going to turn it down. It was a considerable sum and I think Rick was relieved and also a little embarrassed that his cousin had decided to help him out.

Jas hadn't been paying any rent, although he always seemed to have money, especially of late, but if the pending exhibition didn't go well for me, I was going to be leaving Berwick quite soon, and probably in debt.

We left Goathland a couple of hours later and headed back to Berwick. We needed to get back as George's funeral was only a few days away.

Later that week, I watched Liz's pale face and sunken blue eyes as she stood next to her mother at George's grave side. Howard, with his big hearted personality, looked after her and treated her with affectionate kindness and sincere respect. I watched him welcome her into his arms as he told her that he loved her and that he hoped she would be okay. When he'd crossed over the grass, to stand near her on that sultry early summer afternoon, his attention had flattered her. He touched her shoulder, and she smiled. It was the last smile for a very long time.

I let out a sighing gasp of air. I couldn't tell whether it was despairing or simply disbelief.

Across the other side of the grave, behind the throng of mourners, I saw Jas.

I could feel the rage in me rise. *Why the hell was he here?*

He didn't even know George and certainly hadn't been invited to attend the funeral.

Yet again, his uncalled for presence was unbelievable and for me, highly provocative and suspicious.

At that moment, the pall bearers arrived supporting the coffin on their shoulders, and my mind moved away from its state of rage to one of deep sorrow.

We were all silent for a few minutes. A baby was crying somewhere nearby, and I could hear its mother soothing it with a few gentle syllables.

I looked across again at Liz. In the afternoon sun, her face was a set of soft curves, and her blue eyes gleamed with tears.

I did try to find where Jas had moved to and was now standing, thinking he had disappeared behind a group of mourners on the other side of the grave, but then I saw him slinking off along the pathway towards the cemetery gates.

Why he had come, I didn't know but then I didn't want to think about it at that moment.

My attention was drawn back to the funeral party, as the coffin was slowly lowered before it then disappeared into the blackness of the gash that was to be George's final resting place. At that point the stinging hit the back of my eyes as the tears welled up, before running easily down my cheeks. I knew we didn't know half of the reason for George's brutal death. I knew the small daubs of colour that had been excluded from the coroner's summary of the reason for his death were at least as important as the broad strokes that had been included.

I couldn't face the loss of George, my teacher. I hadn't helped to bury him, for God's sake, but I somehow felt responsible for not protecting him. But I didn't grieve, and I

170

didn't mourn him. There wasn't enough truth in me for that kind of sorrowing because my heart wouldn't believe he was dead. I'd loved him as a teacher and a friend. How so much ability and care could vanish into the earth and paint no more, smile no more, then love was nothing. There had to be a pay-off, somehow, and I kept waiting for it. Love, like respect, isn't something you get, it's something you give. But not knowing that in those bitter days, not thinking that, I turned from the hole in my life where so much enjoyment had been, and I refused to feel the longing or the loss.

Jas had left the funeral with the knowledge that all those people that were suspicious of him, were all in one place at the cemetery. He knew that the mini that he had used and had parked down at the dock was going to be found, at some stage. He had stolen some number plates from another car that had been parked in the same area and swapped them over onto the mini. This would give him time he thought.

Apparently acting on this false information concerning the number plates, the police, working from Berwick and the region, concentrated their searches on another area north of the border. For as long as Jas remained part of the community in Berwick, he appeared to be safe. So he waited, trapped and afraid, through the weeks following his heinous crimes. He hid among the people, creeping through their shadows in the daylight hours, and huddled in the hotel bars or pubs most nights, but slowly, one ice-edged day at a time, the knife of his sins whittled the

171

wishing and hoping away until all that was left of him, within the hard, disconsolate wrap of his own arms around his pathetic body, was only the lonely will to survive and prevent being found out, until he could escape and disappear.

The day he killed George had been intense. He accepted the taciturn mood he was in and had been through a strenuous workout exercise in his room, in silence, to ready himself. After a shower, he had asked Rick where Peter was going with George.

"Across to Kelso, Peter said, just by the bridge. He mentioned something about painting a river scene - again."

Rick had said, without looking up from his breakfast bowl.

"Oh, right, yes. Another damn river painting." Jas replied, as he turned to pick up his jacket before returning to his room. He unlocked his bedside cabinet and retrieved a set of car keys that he had kept in there, sadly out of sight.

The Mini, at the time, had been parked close by and after a while had picked it up and cruised along the Kelso road inland and away from the coast. He put the top down and let the breeze of warm air stream through his thick, black hair and loose cotton shirt, like a river of wind. Jas' attention was suddenly taken by seeing Peter on the road by the river, walking towards his Land Rover, parked by the bridge. It had started to rain, so he stopped the car for a minute and closed the roof of the Mini, slipping on a waterproof jacket. He guessed that George would be close by. He drove on a little further then slowed the car down, and pulled over about a hundred metres further on, finding

172

a clearing by some trees. He turned the car around and parked up.

He killed the engine and getting out never took his eyes off Peter.

Now is my chance.

He whispered to himself, bile rising in his gut as his hatred boiled over.

He strolled along the river bank where he suddenly saw some plastic sheeting flapping in the rain and through the other side, a huddled figure. He pulled his thick black hair into a ponytail and removed his watch as he walked.

A quick check showed Peter was inside his Land Rover, the windows steamed up with the moisture from the rain and his body heat, blurring the image of the man inside.

He had taken a baseball bat from the boot of the car. He had bought it sometime ago, from off the internet, so it couldn't be easily traced. The handle fitted his palms perfectly. He walked on through the thick grass on the river bank and crept round the back of the plastic that was protecting George from the rain. George, hearing someone behind, turned and recognised Jas just as he approached.

The attack started without a word. Jas swung the branch wildly, flailing at him and crashing the branch through the plastic in a frenzy and smashing his head. George tried to stand, covering his head with his fists held tightly to his temples. His elbows trying to protect his body. When the fury of the attack abated, George rolled over onto his side, and curled his knees into his chest. He looked up to see Jas as the blood ran into his eyes. Jas made a charge, dropping the branch as George shook his head in fear, as Jas grabbed his arms and dragged him to the edge of the bank where he rolled him into the fast flowing Tweed.

Chapter 17

It was late May, a little more than a few weeks before the exhibition. I was busy making preparations for the coming opening. There was quiet urgency in the work being carried out by the picture framers for both mine and George's paintings. We knew what still needed to be done with regard to invitations, advertising and the production of a catalogue.

Yet there was happiness in the group, and excitement in the easy smiles of all those involved. After all the effort put in, all of us were hungry for the opening.

Liz had been appointed as the person to manage the event and she was responsible for the three days. My role was to assist in the placement and hanging, once the framed pictures had been collected.

All manner of jobs needed to be completed at specific times and Liz was brilliant at organising it all. I was glad to be guided by her and it led to me seeing every corner of the process. She had managed exhibitions of her own pottery before and she seemed at ease, especially as she was still getting over George's murder.

Carmen was always there at her side as well. There was a certain kudos in the roles we had; humble and important tasks were as esteemed in the team as they were sometimes laughed at by others in the wider community in the rowing group. I found myself being rewarded just with love. I only had to lift my head from the work I had been assigned to find myself in a luxuriant garden of Carmen's smiles.

As the manager of the event, Liz was involved in every plan and decision in those preparations. Her authority was clear and unquestioned, but it was a subtle, unobtrusive leadership.

I was lucky to have both her and Carmen in those weeks. Liz visited me at the cottage two and sometimes three times a week, checking on progress of the framing and sharing updates with regard to the catalogue and invitations. Carmen was many at home and concentrating on advertising across the Borders and the Lowlands up to Edinburgh.

Not all the problems were brought to my attention, as Liz managed the resolutions herself quite easily.

Howard had decided that his fancy dress party would be held in his mansion after the weekend of the exhibition, and be as much of a celebration, we hoped, of its success. My invitation sat alongside Rick's on the mantelpiece over the log burner.

Jas had taken his and had squirrelled it away somewhere, probably in his locked bedside cabinet, Rick thought.

The first day of the exhibition finally arrived and I dressed up especially for the occasion. Liz and Carmen were both

175

staying with Howard and we had all spent the previous day at the Town Hall erecting huge presentation boards to hang some pictures from, and sturdy wooden trestle tables along the walls, securing hooks above them for more pictures.

Liz had decided not to split the hall into two sections, but to group both mine and George's work according to vistas. The paintings had been divided into three distinct groups. There were those of the river together and then areas around Berwick and finally, beautiful scenes across the Cheviot Hills.

I had already planned out which pictures were to be grouped together and with some help from Trevor, had spent that afternoon hanging them, although there were many last minute changes in positioning, which was both frustrating and exhausting.

Prominently displayed on a dedicated shelf at the entrance to the Town Hall, was George's last painting, unframed and still taped to his board.

It was surrounded by his brushes and palette.

I noticed an arrangement of sunflowers that Liz had placed there when we had finished.

They were his favourites and unusual in Northumberland where they didn't grow easily.

The final effect was pleasing, we all agreed, and so finally at around eight that evening, we headed for the local Indian Restaurant for dinner and a few pints of Cobra.

Carmen had sent out hundreds of invitations and with the *Berwick Advertiser* providing a free run on promoting the event over two previous weekends, we were confident of a food attendance.

The tourist season had just started and the weather was sunny and warm. Untypical of the area, many had said.

Artists are expected to look the part, I was told, and so with that set firmly in my head, I had found a white collarless cotton shirt and a broad brimmed straw hat. A new pair of caramel coloured chinos finished off the look. I let my shirt tails flap outside my chinos and rolled up my sleeves, gathered my brushes and paint box and headed out.

Rick thought I looked a bit of a "dude", which made us both laugh, as I piled boxes of catalogues into the back of the Land Rover and set off.

Jas hadn't been back the night before and neither of us knew nor cared where he was, although the lack of knowledge surrounding his whereabouts, constantly nagged away at us.

Carmen was standing outside when I arrived.

She was wearing loose silk trousers, a flowing scarf and a long sleeved cotton blouse that looked amazing.

Very French, I thought!

A leather bag sat at her feet and I climbed the steps and knelt to pick it up and held it in my hands for a moment. It too was very French, from Paris, in dark green leather, and a decorative buckle stitched to the side. It was elegant and expensive, but well used. Handing it to her, she smiled, kissed me on the cheek and as she slung it over her shoulder, turned to enter the hall. I watched her lithe body sway gently from side to side with every step, until she reached the doorway where she stopped and turned back, then leant against the pillar and folded her arms. An ironic half smile turned up the corners of her mouth. I smiled as I had often seen. Her long hair was free, and burnished with copper tints by the morning sun. The hazel brown, blazed in her eyes. She was almost too beautiful: as a blush of summer sunrise on a sky wide stream of clouds.

"Are you coming, or are you going to stare at my back all day?" She asked, laughing.

"French women are very obliging when it comes to men admiring their curves," I replied, as Liz arrived and strode past us.

"But, Scottish women can be very obstinate, as I'm sure you are aware," she growled, with a smirk that fluttered just short of a smile. "I've missed you, by the way. We've all been busy and upset, I know, but I need you and I intend to make up for the lost time, as soon as we get this exhibition out of the way."

I was glad that she hadn't forgotten me, but I didn't look her in the eye, even when she unfolded her arms and offered me her hand to take me inside.

We looked around the hall, examining everything with a critical eye. As my gaze followed hers, I saw my paintings alongside those of George, the master.

With her beside me, the space looked amazing.

With her eyes, I saw the light and shade in each painting, the amazing curves of the Tweed, the subtle use of the colours we had both used. I walked all the way round each presentation board then stopped, suddenly.

I looked back to where she now sat on a chair, spraying a little perfume on her wrists.

A rush of pure joy seized me. I was almost overcome that she'd made me see the lovely truth of my work, alongside George's, but I was still feeling unworthy.

"It's too much. I don't deserve to be here. I ..."
"It's fine. Your paintings are just as good. Different, but just as beautiful."
She raised her eyebrows in a high arch as she said it, challenging me to respond and with that gesture it was all right between us. I was so thankful that she thought my work was worthy.
Liz came over, carrying a couple of mugs of coffee. She stared at us both and we stared back at her just as intently, and I was struck by just how happy and relaxed she appeared in just that instance. Happier than I had seen her in weeks. Her deep blue eyes shone and her dimple cheeks rosy, with an expression of interest and humour.
"What are you so happy about, young lady?" I asked her, as a smile appeared across her face as she handed us the mugs.
"I'm so pleased that at last we have the exhibition George always wanted and although its awful that he isn't here to see it, I know he will be pleased. Wherever he is," she said, a little tear appearing in her blue eyes. "And because of you Peter, we have been able to ... I'm so grateful." She sighed, the smile turning to more tears, but they were tears of joy and love.
As Carmen and I held our mugs, Liz wrapped her arms around our shoulders, resting her head on mine. I was big

enough to know that this rare show of affection was a breakthrough with Liz.

At the same time I was small enough to hope that Carmen had noticed it, and was pleased by it.

It was nearly opening time as we chatted about the final roles and duties Liz had given us.

We finished our coffee, and Liz gathered the empty mugs, leaving us alone without a word.

At the door, she gave us a long, lingering smile as she greeted the first couple who had just arrived, as she opened up the hall.

The three days raced past. Each one is as busy as the last. There had been a constant steady flow of invited locals, walk-ins and amazingly several from Edinburgh, who had made it a day trip. Liz had made sure that we had plenty of tea and coffee as well as French bread, cheeses, pate and even shortbread. Passing tourists were dropping by, although not many bought anything.

To my surprise, Carmen had had greeting and birthday cards made up using some of the paintings, which sold out every day.

On the last evening, having locked up the hall, I invited Howard, Trevor, Carmen and Liz back to the cottage and had ordered food from the local Indian Restaurant, as everyone seemed to like it last time. The intention had been to eat on the beach just outside the cottage but it had started to rain. Angus was there with Rick and had bought some beers and sparkling wines.

Howard decided that we would still go ahead and produced an old piece of canvas sail. Angus and Rick set it up as Carmen and Liz spread a plastic sheet underneath and spread the containers on it.

So we all sat beneath the wide canvas sail to eat. I had ordered the food and they delivered it directly to our 'encampment'. Howard and Liz, Rick, Angus and Trevor took their places round the edges of the plastic sheet beside Carmen and me. Rain continued to fall, but the air was warm, and a faint breeze from the bay slowly stirred the humid evening.

Our shelter on the sandy beach beside a few fishing cobbles looked out to the rolling sea. We ate chicken biryani, malai kofta, vegetable korma, rice, curried vegetables, hot naan bread with picked lime chutney.

It was a feast, and the delight that spilled from the eyes of my guests, while they ate their fill, put starlight in their smiles as I watched them.

As the night time fell, the rain stopped and the beer flowed, Rick lit a fire with some drift wood he'd collected. The salt saturated wood, burned with wonderful orange flames until it was time for us all to get to our beds.

Everyone left, except Carmen.

We both looked a bit dishevelled. Her hair was a mess from being in the rain and on the beach and we both smelt of curry and burnt firewood.

We were standing in the doorway to my bedroom when our eyes met, and held. She lingered, watching me expectantly then she stepped close to me and quickly kissed my lips. It was a passionate and generous kiss, one that I had grown to know well, and I let myself slip into her embrace.

Her hands appeared to be trembling as she came into my arms.

I stood there, my chest heaving with a passion that was running in me while my body stood still.

We lay close and warm.

In the darkness, the sand and smokey salt on her arms felt like stardust, and her skin was like a span of night sky.

Her hands were kisses on my skin.

She breathed in murmurs, guiding me, and I spoke rhythm to her, echoing my needs as we enclosed ourselves with rapture and love.

Reflected in my mirror, we were writhing images - mine full of fire from the beach, and hers full of stars. And at last those reflections melted, merged and fused together, as before.

I pressed my lips against her skin and kissed the salt from her as she slowly rolled herself onto my willing body.

Chapter 18

If you stare into its cold dark eye, the camera always mocks you with the truth. The black and white photograph showed all of us at the exhibition assembled for the kind of portrait that makes a group of people, not used to having their photograph taken for the newspaper, seem more stiff and gloweringly self-conscious than they really are. It was impossible to tell from that photo how much that group of friends had loved to laugh, and how readily they had smiled. But none of them were looking directly into the lens of the camera. All the eyes but mine were a little above or little below, a little to the left or a little to the right. Only my own eyes stared back at me as I held the newspaper in my hands, and smiled at each one of them.

The exhibition had gone extremely well as most of George's and many of my own paintings had been sold over the three days. Having the photo in the paper with Liz, Carmen, Howard and I in the front with others behind, including George's last painting in-between us, made me sigh deeply, with both pride and sadness. George would have been pleased, I'm sure.

I had money in the bank. The first time for a good while and I had been promised a couple of commissions, which I was looking forward to starting.

I was sitting in the cafe, where George and I had had breakfast each morning, reading the *Berwick Advertiser,* drinking a cup of strong, freshly brewed coffee when Rick bounded through the door with three large bags.

He had been to the local charity shop to buy some - clothes! We had decided to go to Howard's fancy dress party, which was that night, as "Hells Grannies' ', a throwback to a 1970's comedy act. Although we weren't really bothered what Jas was going to come as, we had sort of decided for him and Rick had agreed to find us all some appropriate long dresses, typically worn by elderly ladies, some hats, cardigans and hand bags. He beamed as he emptied the bags onto my lap, almost spilling my coffee and crumpling the newspaper.

"You've done well." I mused, unravelling the garments as they tumbled out of the bags.

"Sure did," he replied, giggling like a child as he produced hats, dresses and even a couple of purple rinsed wigs.

"These are really fantastic," he continued, putting one of the wigs on, grinning inanely. With his round, gold rimmed glasses, he looked the part, instantly.

I grabbed a fox fur collar and a beanie hat. The staff behind the counter were hysterical, but an elderly couple with pinched, upturned noses were not at all impressed.

Three leather handbags, that had seen better days, sat in the bottom of the third bag. Just to complete the outfits, Rick pulled out of his jacket pocket a pair of extremely wide legged knickers.

"I think *you'll* be wearing those, Rick." I said, raising an eyebrow in mock disgust and moving my head to one side whilst grimacing.

"All we need now is some lipstick, clip-on earrings and some signs to show on our back."

"Signs! What signs?"

"With the words Hell's Grannies, written on them, otherwise no-one will have a clue."

"The vast majority won't have a clue anyway." I retorted, laughing, as his wig slipped to the left, covering one eye.

Just at that moment, looking at the three cotton dresses, with their bright, floral printed patterns, an image of Jas, dressed in one, with his black beard and mane of black hair, made me sit up with a jolt. The difference between all those who had made the exhibition a success and Jas, was so profound, it made my blood boil with anger, deep inside my veins. He was the only person who I could no longer trust nor feel comfortable with being in his presence. The differences between us all, and him, suddenly seemed immense and unconquerable to me - far greater than just a series of suspicious incidents and my dislike of his attitude.

Rick went to get a coffee, while I brooded. The room was warm, but I was cold. My stomach suddenly churned and I couldn't finish my drink.

And then I looked up to see Liz walk into the cafe. Her long, black hair had been cut. The new short style suited her open, honest face, showed off her gorgeous blue eyes and her dimples as she smiled and cupped her new hair style.She was dressed in a pale blue - her favourite colour - a loose blouse and cropped trousers with matching blue

185

sunglasses propped in her thick hair. She looked like a creature of light, a creature made out of the sky and clean, white light.

Without considering what I was doing, I stood and all the clothes and stuff Rick had just bought, tumbled to the floor. She saw me as I approached her. A smile as big as a gambler's promise unveiled her face as she opened her arms to hug me. And then looked at the floor and the pile of old ladies clothes, wigs and hand bags.

"I haven't seen you all week," she said as we sat together and Rick came over with his mug of coffee. "What are all these, Peter?"

"Rick's," I lied, smiling as she picked up the big pair of knickers. "Were you coming in for a coffee? I'll get you one."

It was my excuse to escape and let Rick explain.

"Great," she smiled, putting the knickers into Rick's lap, as he sat down next to her.

"Howard's fancy dress party tonight," Rick explained, sheepishly. "We are going as Hell's Grannies."

"Of course you are," she said slowly, sitting back in her chair and tilting it backwards a little. "And who the hell *are* the Hell's Grannies, Rick?"

"Well, back in the….."

"I don't want to know!" Liz screamed with, and laughed, nearly falling off her tilted chair.

"Actually Liz," Rick suddenly leaned forward and whispered."Have you got any lipstick and some clip-on earrings we can borrow?"

"Lips stick and eye make up I can do, but you're not borrowing my earrings," she said indignantly. "You must have bought these at the charity shop. Didn't you see any there?"

"Didn't look, didn't ask." Rick replied.

"We'll go to the other one on Mary Street. I know the lady who runs it and I'm sure she will have something that will do. Maybe a fake pearl necklace as well?"

"Hey, that would be awesome." Rick shouted as he piled the clothes, bags and other items back into the carry bags, but left his wig still perched, ridiculously, on the top of his head.

I arrived back with her mug of coffee and sat down.

"How's Carmen?" I asked, trying not to appear too eager to know.

"She's cool. You know Carmen. She's got plenty of time on her hands. Misses you. She was really fantastic with all the advertising for the exhibition, you know."

"Oh yes, I certainly do and I am very grateful to everyone and we all made some money out of the whole event too. How are you, Liz?" I asked, watching her face closely, knowing just how hurt she still was, how raw the pain and how sad the whole family was as they continued to deal with their grief.

I stared at her, saying nothing else. She didn't reply to my question.

"Carmen," she explained. "She wants to see you more, very much." She finally said, raising her head and staring back at me. The soil had gone, but the warmth in blue eyes told me everything.

Finishing our coffees, we strolled out into the warm sunshine. The smell of the sea and the gentle breeze were delightful.

I still felt alone though and isolated, when I took in a deep breath and turned to wait for the other two.

People in Berwick were still suspicious of me. Although the police had believed my story around George's death, there were those who obviously thought I was either directly to blame or had some connection to what had happened. The truth was theirs, not mine. For them, the locals came first and were trusted. Those from outside were obviously, therefore the enemy and probably evil. They were the club, the clan and more important and believable than any man or woman that was outside of their community.

Until the murderer was caught, I knew it would always be so.

"I'm just going to take Rick round to the other charity shop. He wants earrings." She wiggled her head mockingly, as if she were wearing her own earrings and showing them off, and laughed.

It shook me out of my dark thoughts and I managed a weak laugh too.

Rick and I followed her down the street and round the corner, to where another charity shop was. It was small and shabby, and the door looked like it could do with a new handle and a repaint.

We shouldered open the door and Liz spoke briefly to the lady behind the counter, who quietly disappeared into a back room, but came back with a wooden box, with ivory inlays. In it were an assortment of inexpensive bits and pieces of costume jewellery.

Liz explained our request, which the lady obviously found quite bizarre, but then offered Rick a double string of fake pearls and a matching pair of clip-on pearl earrings. For me, she had a pair of crimson, satin button earrings and we asked for something big and dangling for Jas. She produced two silver looking spirals, that weren't exactly what elderly grannies might normally wear, but as they were for Jas, we thought they would do, as we didn't really care what they looked like. The whole collection only came to a few pounds, so Rick and I both gave her a tenner, which pleased her no end and we all left happy and rather pleased with ourselves.

That evening we were all getting our "dresses" together. I was to wear a cap sleeved white dress with deep red coloured roses on. The earrings would match. I had the fox fur stole but a sage green hat with a large pin in it. None of us had any appropriate shoes, so we wore our loafers. I had a great handbag that swung dangerously from my arm. Rick, being larger, had to wear a dark blue dress that was ridiculously low cut, but a creamy silk scarf covered his hairy chest up. He wore a beanie hat that looked even more ridiculous on top of his wig. He too had a perfect handbag for swinging. That left Jas with a very long full skirted dress and little waistcoat. It came down, virtually to his ankles. He had decided to tie his hair back, which with his beard and big spirally earrings, looked completely, NOT, like a granny.

We had sewn a white handkerchief to the back of each dress and written the words "Hell's Granny" on each one, in black ink.

Liz said she would drop by, to apply both lipstick and eye shadow, so we all sat round the table to wait for her to arrive.

It was quiet until Jas suddenly spoke.

"Who are your friends here?" he asked me. The question surprised me, and I couldn't guess at his intention. Reading my baffled expression, and clearly amused, he asked me again. "Of those you have come to know here, in Berwick, who are your friends?"

"Well, Howard and Rick, obviously, and Liz...."

"So, Liz is your friend now?"

"Yeah," I laughed. "Of course, she's a friend. And I like Trevor and Angus. Then there is Carmen, who is gorgeous."

Jas nodded as I went through the list, but when he made no comment I felt moved to speak again.

"They are *all* good people, I think. But those...those are the ones I get on with the best. Is that what you mean?"

"What about George?"

"Yes, I believe George was a good friend as well, but....."

"Who is your favourite now?" He asked, slightly changing the focus unexpectedly.

"My favourite... It's a crazy question."

"No it's not. It's an easy question. It must be Carmen."

"No, Jas. She is more than a friend. And you fucking know that she is, so what's your point?"

He smiled, but the smile twisted into a sneer. I was sure, somehow, that there was something more sinister about his questioning and I didn't like the fact that he had mentioned Carmen.

"What about me?" He suddenly asked, looking down at his nails as he picked at them.

"What about *you*?"

Rick, sat up and quietly coughed.

"I wonder where Liz is?" He said standing up and obviously wanting to change the subject. "She said she would be here before seven and it's already ten past."

Jas got up and came over to my side.

"I understand," he murmured, reading my eyes. "Tell me, when the others are not around. I'll ask you again when we are alone and so you can tell me the truth."

"I'm .... Not really sure what I think about you Jas," I replied, frowning. I got off my chair, not because I needed to, but for the distraction it provided.

"What are you thinking now, as you look into my eyes?" He asked, annoyed that I had moved.

"I couldn't possibly say, as I think about lots of things and people mostly, I think about people I love and trust. I think about people who have died.... Recently. I remember friends, and people I love."

"But you haven't answered my question, Peter."

I was saved from having to tell Jas what I really thought of him, when Liz and Carmen knocked on the front door and walked in. The stunned look on their faces when they saw us in our dresses, was one of wide eyed astonishment, followed by howls of laughter.

Together, they applied bright postbox red lipstick to each of our puckered mouths. Carmen thought it very funny to apply a much thicker and wider amount, to my lips, for some reason, that only she found hysterically amusing.

Viridian green eye shadow completed our 'look', and when I passed the mirror in the hall on the way out and caught sight of my own *new* reflection, I thought for a second, just one tiny second, that I could actually pass, just possibly, as a refined elderly lady.

Although we decided to drive up to Howard's, we knew that a taxi home would have to be our transport back and needed to be ordered, unless we managed to somehow persuade Howard to let us stay overnight.

Howard's mansion looked stunning as we drove up its long drive. The whole facade was brilliantly illuminated. People were in the grounds and gardens. Inside they celebrated with dancing and drinking because, when we had succeeded so well with the exhibition, local people had really enjoyed the experience and I think felt genuinely pleased that George's work had been prominent.

I danced and drank with Carmen and friends that evening. The array of different fancy dress costumes were wonderful. Carmen and Liz had waited until we had got to Howard's before they changed into their costumes. The two of them had decided to dress as the *two ugly sisters* from Cinderella, who in actual fact were the victims in this classic story and called Drizella and Anastasia Tremaine the so-called "ugly" and "evil" stepsisters.

When I explained this to them they were more concerned as to who I thought was the ugly one and who was the evil one !!

Throughout the evening whenever I looked at Carmen, she smiled every time I turned my hungry eyes on her. I was in love with her, and even if she had been lazy or a coward or miserly or bad-tempered I would have loved her still. But she was brave, compassionate and generous. She worked hard, and she was more than a good friend. That night I found new ways and reasons to like the woman I had already loved with all my heart.

The one strange and yet amusing event that seems to occur quite often, was that many of the other women at the party seemed to think, albeit in some case, only for a couple of minutes, that the *Hell's Grannies* were actually elderly ladies, grannies, women. I think the dimmed lights, plenty of sparkling wine and the sheer madness that is fancy dress, helped a great deal in this illusion, but Rick and I did indeed find ourselves being opening invited to join other "ladies" to come powder their noses with them until suddenly realising that we were of course in fact - men and were not only verbally abused but physically attacked as well. On these occasions, we found that our handbags became very useful defensive weapons.

It was late when most seemed to have had enough to drink and the dancing had become too arduous. Sitting on the mansion steps saying goodnight to people made us realise, we too needed to wind the evening down.

A couple staggered past us. Rick and Angus, along with Carmen and I were looking up at the stars and chatting when they passed.

"You guys were very naughty tonight," The young, rather intoxicated woman said as her boyfriend helped her down the steps. "But weren't there three of you earlier on. You two and an Indian chap, with a beard. Now he really was naughty." She continued, swaying and grabbing hold of her boyfriend's arm as she just about managed another step.

"What do you mean?" Rick asked, suddenly concerned.

"Think he was giving one of the *Ugly Sisters* a good humping in one of the bathrooms. Really one hell of a sight. Didn't expect to see what looked like an old woman, shagging another, and younger woman. Anyway, good night all. Great party. See you around....." Her boyfriend announced, waving his free arm and hand about, whilst thrusting his groyne forward with exaggerated menace to demonstrate what he had just described.

And with that parting comment, they wandered off down the long driveway towards the gates.

I looked at Carmen and then Rick. We all came to the same awful conclusion at the same time.

The party was in full swing soon after he and the rest had arrived, with plenty to eat and drink. The music had got everyone on their feet. Well, almost everyone. Jas watched Liz from some distance away. He could see Peter and Carmen dancing near the French doors, surrounded by his *friends*. Liz was approaching them with slow dance steps in tune with the beat.

194

Jas thought she looked hot, even dressed up as the ugly sister from Cinderella. She stood with the group and Howard slipped an arm around her.

Fucking bastard. Should have finished you off on the road that night. He said to himself, taking a sup from his glass and watching the group still.

The guests in the room were all dancing out their best moves with near hysterical enthusiasm for the music. Some of them adopted poses of their favourite singer or musician, and copied the dance steps of the stars. Others left about like drunken acrobats, or invented jerky, exuberant dances of their own.

Jas thought they all looked and behaved like self righteous bastards.

Listening to the music and watching the dancers, his mind wandered back to Liz, and he thought of how he would like to abuse her. He watched her like a cat would watch a mouse before it pounced. He wanted to capture the trusting creature, and fuck her, face down arms stretched as if being crucified, on a cross made from splintered wood. He laughed to himself as he imagined how she would struggle when he had tied her by her neck to the cross with her own ribbons from her dress. He marvelled at his developing plan and how, dressed as a "granny", he would be able to sneak past other women and surprise Liz before she realised. Other people wouldn't recognise him dressed up, and anyway, most of them were too drunk to notice who was next to them.

Are we ever justified in what we do?

That question ruined the creeping delight in his mind, but only for a minute or two.

Jas looked at Liz again, gyrating and drunk and thought of how his sick plan would play out.

Would her trusting innocence be sized by fate that couldn't have been hers without me, without my intervention in her life?

What wounds and torments awaited Liz simply because I had befriended her and she trusted me.

Jas watched and heard her shout across to Carmen, saying that she was going for a pee, and pointed to the ceiling, indicating she was heading for one of the bathrooms on the first floor.

Jas couldn't resist the call to follow her. He left his leaning post at the door and joined the thick tangle of jerking, writhing bodies on the dance floor. Stumbling between the dancers, he skipped to the other side of the room, just as Liz was leaving. He reached the other door and watched her start up the stairs.

He turned for a moment to see if anyone was watching him. Peter, and his friends, were too drawn into the avalanche of revelry to notice and Jas watched him for a while, glide and sway gracefully around with Carmen in his arms, before he chased up the stairs to find which bathroom Liz had gone into.

It didn't take long as she was in the first one he came to.

Bending over a little and hiding his face, he quietly closed the door. Liz was adjusting her skirt and was looking in the mirror. He drew near to her but just outside her vision.

Liz stopped and looked at the reflection of herself and Jas in the mirror. He grinned at her until the grin became a

196

sneering laugh. He lifted Liz off her feet and easily turned her round before slamming her over the bathtub, wrenching at her skirt.

"You look fucking great, Liz," he laughed. "Now you can enjoy this."

He held her head down, tied his thin scarf around her head and mouth to stop her from screaming, whilst he hitched up his own skirt, took out his penis and climbed on to the back of her, trying to thrust it into her. His hand ripping at her writhing body.

Suddenly, the door opened and a couple walked in, giggling and drunk.

They saw the back of Jas in his dress and wig, wedged over Liz.

"Whoops, sooorrry," a man's voice said as he pulled the woman he had with him back out of the bathroom.

"Didn't mean to interrupt you both." He laughed, closing the door.

Jas heard them laughing as they left. It must have been a strange sight, but at least they didn't see who it was, he hoped.

The interruption had been enough for Liz to rid herself of her rapist, but just as she managed to turn around, she was struck across her left cheek which knocked her back against the rim of the bath.

Jas beat her around the head with his fists, in a frenzied attack. He was drunk, and he beat her terribly.

He left her on the bathroom floor, covered in blood and unconscious.

He was annoyed that the couple had robbed him of his initial intent, and as he was angry and drunk, thought he had better get out of there. Taking the key from the door, he closed it quietly, locking it from the outside before tossing the key into a plant pot, sitting on a stand, at the top of the landing, and walked quickly to the staircase and down to rejoin the party.

"What did that couple say?" Angus asked, turning and pointing in their direction as they disappeared into the darkness of the driveway.

Carmen suddenly wrapped her arms around me, but I just suddenly felt very numb.

"That could only be Jas, with someone," I said to Carmen, as she looked back at me with a little fear in her eyes.

"Where's Liz?" I suddenly said, raising my voice as my heart beat trebled.

"Where the hell is Liz?" I asked the others.

"Haven't seen her for a couple of hours, what the hell. It's a party." Rick replied, questioning my thinking, but sobering up rather quickly when he realised what I was asking.

Getting up, we half ran back into the house, first into the dance hall. There were few people left there and Liz wasn't there.

"Let's split up." Carmen screamed and dragged me out of the room.

"She's not in here." We heard Rick shout from somewhere further back on the mansion.

"That couple said they saw two people in a bathroom."

There was a sudden pain in my chest, right next to my heart, and I breathed in, and out, and in. Carmen took my hand and we rushed upstairs to find the first bathroom door locked.

"Hey, is there anyone there?" I shouted, hammering on the door. I heard a muffled sound and crying.

"Liz... Liz, are you in there?"

The sobbing grew louder as I tried to force the door open.

Carmen had rushed to the top of the stairs and was shouting at the others to come up. A crowd of bodies stormed up the stairs and together we broke open the door. Lying in a pool of blood, was Liz.

"Ah, Jesus," I moaned."Ah, fuck. Ah, God."

"Liz!" Carmen rushed to help her.

"I'll call the police," Rick said, quiet and confident."They'll find out what happened. But we'll find..... him. We'll find you Jas, you fucker."

Carmen collapsed by Liz's side. I rubbed the tears out of my eyes with the heels of my hands.

"It's a terrible thing," Angus said

"Yeah."

"It shouldn't have happened."

"No."

"And it didn't need to have happened. Not this."

"He didn't need to take it that far. She hadn't done anything to him."

"What do you mean - needn't have taken it *that far?*" Carmen screamed at Angus. "He's half beaten her to death and by the looks her, he raped her first." She continued, looking at him with a frown that was so angry in its bewilderment.

I called out to Rick who was on the phone to the emergency services and told him to get an ambulance here, first.

Carmen had lifted Liz up a little.

"Oh, my God, Peter," she said, the blood on Liz's face trickling down to her throat.

Carmen's voice cracked, and her eyes filled with tears.

"She's been beaten about the head. We need to get her to a hospital." She said and wept openly.

"She's hurt - very badly hurt, Rick. She needs an ambulance now… I just hope that…..'

I broke down too and wept. Bringing myself under control only with deep breaths and a clenched jaw effort of will.

I reached out to comfort Carmen as Liz was now conscious but obviously in a lot of pain.

"How bad is it?" Rick asked as he came into the bathroom.

"Both the police and the ambulance are on their way. Just a couple of minutes away, they said."

The paramedic said he was sure she wasn't going to die. A comforting thought !

They put bandages around her head and a drip in her arm and quickly manoeuvred her out, on a stretcher, and into the waiting ambulance. The blue flashing light bounced eerily off the huge pillars outside Howard's mansion.

The police arrived at the same time. When they saw and recognised me, albeit with a dress on, but having discarded both fox fur and wig, I knew I would be the first to be questioned.

Chapter 19

The police had rounded up all the remaining guests who were still in the house and a search of the house and surrounding area had started, once the police had been informed that the suspected attacker was probably still in the grounds of Howard's mansion.

Several more police cars had arrived once the ambulance had sped away. Sirens blaring and blue lights everywhere. We never thought there were that many in the whole of the Borders force, let alone Berwick!

Jas watched it disappear down the driveway as he hid amongst the laurel bushes near the main gates of the house. He had been hiding there ever since he had left the house and worked his way past several unsuspecting guests, with the intent on escaping down the driveway and out along the road when he had the chance, when he had heard a siren in the distance, before seeing the blue flashing lights of the ambulance as it swerved in through the open gates, followed by a police car.

Once they had both passed by, he ran out onto the main road and headed for Berwick, although it wasn't long before a large police Range Rover, seeing a figure in the road, slowed down. The two officers saw the dark shape walking along the side of the road, but seeing the clothing and the hunched figure, thought it was an old woman.

Quickly he covered his face and head with his shawl. The wig and hat that he had retained, and his long "granny" dress covered the rest of him quite adequately. He bent over to make himself look smaller and older.

Clutching the leather handbag in front of himself, he slowed a little and walked with a limp, giving the impression that he was indeed an elderly lady.

The police vehicle stopped alongside him and the passenger window was lowered. They shone a torch on the figure, but seeing the shawl over the hat and wig, they assumed it was a little old lady.

"Are you okay there madam? You are out a wee bit late." A gruff Scottish accent came from the policeman in the front passenger seat.

Jas put on an accent and tried to speak with a lighter voice, to sound like an old lady.

"Aye, thank ye constable, just been te see an ol' friend in Tweedmouth." He said, quite convincingly.

"Ye have ne seen a young man along this road then?" He asked the figure in the shawl.

"No' this evening, but lots o'cars though." Jas said, keeping his head down and the handbag close to his chest.

"Well, get ye self home quick there missus. It's late and the road's dark."

Jas thanked him as the window closed and the Range Rover sped off, leaving him breathing heavily and trembling a little.

Once they were out of the way, he jumped off the road and scrambled down the bank into the bushes before climbing a post and rail fence, ripping his dress as he did. Once safely on the other side and well out of sight, he laughed as he peeled back the shawl and laid back in the long grass. The evening was warm and the sky was clear. The stars shone as he looked up at them and smiled.

He was pleased that he had so easily fooled everybody and especially the police. His costume and the darkness of the unlit road had surely saved him from being caught.

"Stupid fuckers!" He murmured to himself as he listened to his beating heart whilst rubbing frantically, at the dried remains of Liz's blood on his bruised fists.

"It's fucking *great!*" he laughed. "I escaped from all you fuckers, and beat the shit out of her too after giving her a good doing. It's the greatest thing I've ever done. It's tearing my heart out that I can't tell anyone about it."

The bitterness in his voice was disconcerting. His jaw began to set in a grim and angry expression as he stared at his bloodied hands. His dark brown eyes glistened as he ran a hand over his face and up across his forehead, removing the wig and hat.

He lay there and recalled his brutal attack on Liz. Using her grip on the tie of the bath as leverage, he had smashed her head onto the taps, three, four, five times and then punched her cheek with his fist as she tried to pull away. He had enjoyed violating her before the beating and remembered tasting her blood, as she thrashed wildly until his last blow knocked her unconscious.

He was sick with jealousy and rage.

He knew that this time, he would need to get away from Berwick. He had to get some different clothes, which meant going back to the cottage. That could be a problem, but he then needed to reach the mini parked in the dockyard, and then perhaps drive north, maybe to Edinburgh. He wondered if Carmen's house would be a good place. He knew where it was and as she was at Howard's for the

204

foreseeable future, he could drive up there, break in easily, wait for her to get back and then decide what further action he would need to take.

The police drove us to the hospital and on our arrival I found the doctor in charge of her care. I had left Carmen at Howard's as she was exhausted. She had run too much and so we put her to bed before Rick and I left after some initial questioning. With everyone else's information, I had suddenly become reliable enough to leave.

She was badly beaten, he said, but he wasn't sure how badly hurt she was until she had been x-rayed. There was nothing we could do for her except wait until she had been fully examined. I returned to the waiting room and joined Rick, we were both still a little drunk and like Carmen, exhausted.

I found a toilet in the hospital and then washed my face and neck. The cold water felt good on my aching head with the thoughts of Liz and too much alcohol. I couldn't bare to think those thoughts. I couldn't hold the image of our beautiful friend Liz being beaten by a maniac, until her body was beaten and bloodied. I stared into the mirror, feeling the acid burn of tears. I slapped myself hard awake, and returned to the waiting room. Rick was asleep, slumped in a chair. I left him there.

An hour or so later I was still sitting in the room with Rick. I was so tired, I began to nod off, and I had to admit that I couldn't stay awake. In a relatively quiet corner, I put two chairs against the wall and went to sleep. A dream swallowed me whole, almost at once. It carried me to the

Tweed, and to the place where George had been beaten unconscious, and thrown into the water, and left to drown. I was floating on the murmuring tide of voices. His and mine. He had put his hand on my shoulder and praised my work, and we had laughed together. When I woke from the dream, Rick was sitting there beside me with *his* hand on my shoulder, and when I met his eyes we both knew that Jas had done this to Liz and that he needed to be stopped.

We heard the doctor's voice coming down the corridor, he was talking with a nurse as he walked into the waiting room.

"Gentlemen!" the voice said. "Thank you for waiting so long, I have some news about the patient. She can't open her left eyelid due to the swelling and severe bruising, and she has several lacerations to her head, but you can come and see her for a short visit, as the police are here and want to interview her."

I brought my face close to hers, so I could talk to her quietly.

Her mouth was cut, and her cheek was swollen along with her left eye. The other was bloodshot, but half open and she could see me, perhaps. Other punches had landed on her temple and her head was bandaged where it seems she had needed stitches. She smiled. You can never tell just how much pain there is in a person until you see them smile.

"Luckily, her left eye is intact but the socket is fractured and she needed several stitches to her forehead,"the doctor informed us, in a matter-of-fact tone. "There are no other *serious* issues thank goodness. I gather that the perpetrator may well have been, "interrupted", during the attack,

206

which might just have saved her from far more serious injuries. She has some other physical damage, but that information, I am afraid, is confidential as she has yet to be interviewed by the police. Sorry, I can't tell you any more."

With that, he marched out of the room and left Rick and I alone with her, under the watchful eye of the duty nurse.

"Miss, you must take your medicine first."

The nurse brushed past us as we watched her administer some tablets. She gave her a sip of water. The drip in her arm suggested she was being given something else, a little stronger, no doubt. We watched her lips part, and the water flow into her mouth along with the tablets. She swallowed with difficulty, gulping and spluttering. She closed her right eye and we realised that she was in no state to talk.

At least she was alive, which was miraculous under the circumstances, and was now being looked after and obviously in safe hands. We got up to leave, just as a police woman entered the private room Liz had been put in, as much for her own security, she said, rather than for any medical reasons.

The dawn was just breaking as we tried to get Howard to answer his mobile. He didn't, and neither did Carmen when I rang her number.

It was going to be a long journey home and a long time getting there. Neither of us had any money, nor means of getting back home, without transport or help.

Later that afternoon, having managed to hitch-hike our way back to Tweedmouth, we walked up the drive back to Howard's. I asked myself a thousand times, through those

207

hours, whether we could have done more to stop all this from happening sooner.

We arrived at the house and they were sitting there, in that massive room, feeling the tinge of guilt. Carmen smiled. A thin lipped smile. I knew that they had all been talking once the police had interviewed them all. I had managed to connect with Carmen earlier and let her know how Liz had been. And while a discussion took place around us, I spoke the words, quite clearly, in the secret voice of prayer and incantation.....*We'll get you, we'll get you, we will get you...*

"Peter, you're not listening to the discussion? " I suddenly heard Howard saying to me.

"Please, permit us to hear what your muttering wisdom is about? You are blaming Jas, I know, but I did say to you, let the police handle this." He said, curtly.

"I have been told by some, that this... this act of barbaric and brutal behaviour, this sin and wrongdoing is the cause of his suffering, isn't that right?"

Rick shook his head in disagreement, his gleaming eyes nesting under his tufted eyebrows, where his glasses nestled. He seemed agitated about what I was saying and turned away.

"Living by right principles, according to the teachings of all religions, will banish suffering from the life of a good person. Am I correct?"

"Where are you going with this?" Howard cut in, impatiently. "None of us will disagree with your argument about that, but aren't you being a bit extreme? I remember not so long ago you were happily laying into people in the pub because they thought *you* were the killer. It is of course true that we should have a touch of sympathy for someone who is quite obviously mentally disturbed, it's only human, but what the hell is all this talk of his suffering?"

No one spoke or moved. There was a perceptible sharpening of focus and attention in the few silent moments as I gathered my thoughts. Each person in that room had their own opinion and level of articulacy, yet I had the clear impression that Howard's contribution was usually the last word. I sensed that his response would set the tone. His expression was impassive, and his eyes were cast down, trying to avoid my stare, but he was far too intelligent not to perceive the awe he inspired in others. When I had got to know him better, I discovered that he was always avidly interested in what others thought of him, always aware of his own charisma and its effects on those around him, but I wasn't gonna let him wash over the fact that Jas was a killer, and that some of the things that had happened, were mere accidents, chances, or anything but a calculating, murdering albeit, sick man.

"My belief, and I think that of others here, is that Jas killed both Lisa and George, attempted to kill you Howard, by running you off the road, attempted to suffocate Rick by cutting his air supply, and has also just tried to kill Liz after raping her, and..." I continued, putting my hand up to prevent Howard from cutting in again. "And, Rick and I, with anyone else who thinks similarly, are going to find him and get the truth from him. One way or another. Does anyone wish to discuss this point before we proceed?"

I looked from one face to another. Some people nodded grimly in appreciation of my point, some nodded their agreement, some others frowned in concentration, and one , Howard, in disagreement.

"Right then. Enough is enough. Rick and I are going to head back to Crab Cottage. If Jas isn't there, then we'll start to look for him. Unless he has some other clothes already, an Indian with a beard dressed as an elderly lady can't be that hard to find." I was beginning to get quite boisterous, when Rick intervened.

"The white mini that nearly knocked you off the road Howard. It might be the one Peter and I found in the dock yard in Spittal. Different number plate than the one Peter saw at the bridge in Kelso, but it may well have been swapped over."

"You see!" Howard said, jumping to his feet, clenching his fists to his sides. "That's what I mean. You don't know what you're doing. Leave it to the police to investigate."

"We have already informed them twice and have found, or even done anything about it…. No?" I said, right in Howard's face. "I trust you didn't have any input into the lack…*investigations,* by the police, did you Howard ?"

The other's all shook their heads, not understanding really what was going on.

Chapter 20

I stood with Rick and Carmen at the back wall of the boat house in the dockyard. Behind us was a sealed door that Jas had hidden behind. In front of us was a line of cars, one of them being the white, soft top Mini that we suspected Jas had been driving. We were all quite shocked that we had found ourselves there, despite the openness of the area and people all around.

"So what do you think?" Rick whispered.

"It's incredible?" I replied, my eyes gleaming in the soft light of the shaded lamps in the yard. Carmen felt exhilarated, and perhaps a little unnerved.

We had all had a couple of gins before and perhaps they had relaxed the muscles of her face and shoulders, but there were tigers moving quickly in the eyes of her soft smile.

"It's frightening. It's horrible and yet right at the same time. I can't make up my mind which is the right part, and which is the horrible part. Horrible - that's not the right word, but it's something like that."

"I know what you mean," I agreed, thrilled that we had tracked Jas down.

My tone implied that I was calm and ready, the truth was the complete opposite.

One of the fishermen came out and approached us slowly with his fishing rod.

He was a friend of Angus, who was waiting inside, and was tall and lean, but his muscles were thick and I watched them ripple in the lamp light. He had deep valleys that ran from his temples to a hard and hungry jaw. His eyes were huge, within the caverns ridged by his brows, and there was a look of fearlessness.

Angus had seen Jas sneaking round the back of the shipyard. He had obviously got back to the cottage and changed but he was coming for the car, when Angus had seen him from the rowing club and phoned me.

Racing up from the cottage in my Land Rover wasn't probably the subtlest way to arrive, but we couldn't let him escape, not this time.

The fisherman told us that Angus intended to flush Jas out and for us to be ready. So we waited as the fisherman turned and stood off, with his back towards the doors, muttering about us in a soft drone.

A scream suddenly pierced the air. We all turned to the street entrance gate to the dock yard. A man dressed in a red turban, vest, and jeans stood there, near the iron gates, shrieking at the very top of a strong voice.

Before we could discern what he was saying or react, the man drew a long, thick bladed sword and raised it over his head.

Still screaming, he began to walk towards the cars that were parked in the yard. He was staring directly at Carmen as he walked, with a stomping, marching tread. I couldn't understand the words he was screeching, but I knew what he had in mind. He wanted to attack her. He wanted to kill her.

We flattened our backs against the walls instinctively. The door behind us was still locked shut. There was no escape. We were unarmed.

The man walked on towards us, waving the sword in circles over his head with both hands.

There was nowhere to go, and nothing to do, but to fight him. I took one step to the side to protect Carmen, and raised my fist. The door behind us suddenly opened and out stepped the fisherman and Angus. I felt good about it and was so relieved that I almost fainted.

Like every other tough, angry man I had known, he scared me ridged.

At the last possible moment, the fisherman had emerged from the shadows, tripped the red turbaned swordsman, and sent him crashing to the floor. The sword fell from his hand and clattered to a stop at Carmen's feet. She snatched it up, and we watched as the man who had tripped up our assailant tried to grab hold of him, but the man twisted away and seconds later was looking up into my face.

It was Jas.

Carmen saw him too and her eyes burned. She hesitated before raising the sword. It was too late. Jas escaped, running down to the river. I thought he was going to the car, but he ran past it and disappeared behind the buildings.

In the confusion that followed his departure, I checked on Carmen. Her eyes were wide and she pursed her lips with anger, but she wasn't distressed. Reassured, I went to thank the man who had stepped in to help us.

"I owe you," I said, giving him a smile that was as cautious as it was grateful. He'd moved with such lethal grace that he made the disarming of Jas seem effortless. I knew how much skill and courage it had taken, and how big a role instinct had played in his timing.

Angus came out and when we turned to follow Jas, the fisherman was already gone.

The dockyard was deserted.

I checked on the Mini. It was still there with nobody inside. Wherever Jas was, he couldn't be too far away. We ran over to where I had parked up and climbed in and headed off to Berwick.

Carmen and Rick were silent during the ride, and I too said nothing, annoyed that our attempt to catch Jas had failed and had ended in such confusion and near disaster. Only Angus felt free to speak.

"What a lucky escape!" He said, from the front seat grinning at me. "I thought Jas was going to chop us up in teeny pieces. Hell, he really does have a screw or two, loose."

At the High Street, we got out of the Land Rover and stood searching for any sign of Jas.

"Let's split up ?"

"You coming with me?"

"No," I answered, wishing I was sounding more confident than I felt. "I'm staying with Carmen. You and Rick head towards the walls and we'll start looking round here."

We were facing the sea, looking down on a section of the river. An ice cream vendor tried to sell us a cone each. Carmen turned to look the other way.

"What is it?" I asked, wondering why she had suddenly turned to look up the road.

"I don't know, just a hunch maybe. He needs to escape from here. Maybe he's heading for the railway station." She said, and stared into my eyes for a moment.

"Sounds a good place to start." I said as we both began to jog up the hill towards the station.

We arrived at the station quickly and strode round the corner onto platform one.

There, pacing up and down was Jas.

As we approached, my heart started beating , wondering what I would say, wondering what he would do.

He saw us and stopped.

"Hats pretty fucking good," Jas mused, grinning, "So you found me so quick. I'm losing today, man. It's this passion thing. It's driving me insane, Peter. Oh yeah, everyone loves you don't they, but I'm the one that really cares. You were always with the others, fucking others, cheating on me, doing the painting stuff and fucking her."

Jas was ranting and Carmen and I didn't know what to say.

"But I haven't done anything to you Jas, have I?"

"You were friends with Rick right from the start, then Howard and your old man painter. All the time fucking her." He said, pointing at Carmen.

"Oh, come on, Jas! You really think I liked everyone but you. That's it, that's what all this carnage has been about?"

Jas' eyes widened in surprise, and then narrowed into an evil frown. He picked at his jacket.

"You know, Peter, we've been together here for quite a while now, living and working in Berwick, and met and loved lots of people and even fucked the women and all, but you still don't get it do you?"

"Maybe not," I conceded."Probably not."

"Damn right you don't, man. This is Britain man, the land of my heart. This is where my heart is king and I am free to do what I want. To love who I want. That's why I can walk around and pick up who I want. I could have fucked you, Peter. I could have loved you, and fucked you, and taken your money. I could have taken your money for fucking you and then let all the others live, but you didn't want me. There's no love in you, there's no heart in you, for me."

He was crying. Stunned, I watched him wipe the tears from his eyes.

"You think I'm crazy don't you?"

"No, but I think you needed help and you needed to realise that I am not like you."

"I haven't really figured out what exactly has been happening. I did forgive them, I really did. And I'm sure, somehow, that's what drove me on. I don't mean that I stopped being angry-shit, if I'd gotten a gun, I probably would have killed them all. Or maybe not. I don't know. But I hated them - if I hadn't hated them then I would have hated you. My hate would have killed *you*."

He turned to look at me, his eyes gleaming, and there was a broken smile fixed on his face.

"My hate for them is what saved you, Peter," he said quietly, but with an excited, feverish zeal.

"My hate got stronger and harder. And here it is now inside me, where it belongs. And I'm glad. I enjoy it. I need it, Peter. I'm stronger than my love for you now. I'm braver than I was then and my hate is now my hero."

He held that fanatic stare for a moment, and then turned to Carmen.

"Challo Bhai!" he snapped. "And, I hate you the most!"

A second later he was running along the platform and onto the side of the railway lines, heading along the viaduct.

I shouted at him to stop and wait, but he kept running. Carmen and I set off after him but he'd surprised us and had a head start. He was wearing black, a black vest, trousers and trainers, which all looked strange with his red turban that we had never seen him wear before. He stumbled along running in between the sleepers. A quick look round made him realise that we were gaining on him.

Finally, I caught up and ran at him and rammed a fist into his back, but it didn't seem to have any effect.

He suddenly stopped and turned and I heard a frightened shriek as he thrust his right-hand at my throat. I held his vest with my left hand, and pointed at him with my right. Ignoring the blows to his head, he managed to get his hands around my neck, and started to squeeze.

My throat locked tight. I knew that the breath I held in me was the last until I finished him. I reached out for his face, when suddenly his grasp was ripped from my throat.

Carmen had swung a fist at his head.

She didn't find it easy to knock him out and he sat on the edge of the viaduct parapet, and away from us.

"Yeah, *you* fucking understand?" Jas shouted at her, lashing out with a kick to keep us away. "You come any closer and I will finish you as well."

"You ruined my life." He screamed at her and with one deft move, threw one leg over and then the other, and then was suddenly gone.

Carmen and I stood there for what seemed an age before realising that Jas had just dropped himself over the edge of the viaduct. There had been no noise, no screaming, no sound at all but the wind blowing up the Tweed.

Neither of us moved until we heard shouting from behind us.Turning around, and still stunned by what had we had just witnessed, we saw a railway man, in a high-vis jacket

218

and two policemen, one trying to hold his cap on, running and tripping their way along the viaduct towards us.

Chapter 21

We passed beneath the archway and the trees and into the soft afternoon light to meet Liz. She was crying. Carmen was crying. Carmen threw herself forward and wrapped her in her arms. She kissed her on her cheek. Liz's face was still bruised and the stitches hadn't been removed yet, but she was happy and she looked well, under the circumstances. I watched them for a moment and then I turned away to see Rick coming up behind us. He grinned at me, and walked with a jaunty swagger. I did a little victory dance for no apparent reason.

On the day, an hour after Jas' confession to me and Carmen, I let the screaming hatred fade. Right or wrong. I didn't want to think about the reasons for Jas doing what he did, or what he felt about me. I didn't really want his truth nor his confession, and I couldn't face it. So the thoughts and premonitions echoed and then whipped past me in that warm sea breeze.

Today was a new beginning for us all and we were going to celebrate, initially Liz's homecoming from the hospital. By the time we had walked to the last curve of the river near the Sea Horse Hotel, my mind was as clear as the broad horizon clamped upon the limit of a dark and tremulous sea.

Jas had committed his last act of hatred on himself when he jumped from the viaduct. The fall had killed him and the tide had taken him out to sea before the rescue teams could find and recover his body.

The SeaHorse, which was as luxurious and opulent as the other hotels in Berwick, offered a decent enough lunch and as well as the special attraction that it was literally built upon the sea rocks. We decided to have the comprehensively eclectic smorgasbord lunch. I was hungry and glad to see that Liz and Carmen were too. Carmen looked beautiful in her starched, sky-blue shirt with the collar turned up, and sky blue culottes. His dark hair was wound into the praying fingers of a French braid. She looked tanned and healthy and confident.

Liz wore tight jeans and a red T-shirt. The white bandages reminded me of a turban. The memory of Jas' red turban on his last day, flashed through my mind.

We all piled into the restaurant. A young woman with a short haircut, carrying a pad approached us, handing out menus.

"Great, I'm starving." Rick said, handing back the menu and ordering the smorgasbord for all of us.

That evening, back in Crab Cottage, Carmen and I were talking. Rick had gone to bed to read. We had discussed how the RNLI had found the body, the next day a few miles down the coast. The police said that they had seen him jump, so we weren't implicated in his suicide.

"You know that he did all those things, Peter, and still you blame yourself, is that it?" Carmen asked me.

"Something like that."

"You heard what he said about hating everyone that …. loved you. He was in love with you. That was the problem. And if you must know," she said softly, her voice emptied of all its French emotion, "I'm in love with you too."

I clamped my jaw shut, listening to the ruffle of air breathing in and out through my nose, until our two patterns of breath matched one another in rhythmic rise and fall.

"And what about you? She asked, at last, her eyes closing more slowly and opening less often."You've got my thoughts. When are you going to tell me your thoughts?"

I let the raining silence close her eyes. She slept. I knew how much I loved her. I knew the huge daubs of colour she brought into my life and painted with broad brush strokes brilliantly. The devil had nearly taken her away from me, but despite all that had happened around us, she had given me a hoard of wonderful treasures. Lovers find their way by such gifts. They are the stars we use to navigate the ocean of desires.

I left her to sleep and wondering whether Rick was also asleep, quietly opened his door. He was still reading.

"Hey, Rick. Can I have a word?" I said in a loud whisper, not wanting to wake Carmen.

"What about? It's late Peter."

"The notebook Jas used to write stuff in. The one you found in his bedroom."

"What about it?"

"When the police came round to search his room, they didn't find it. They broke open the bedside cabinet but found nothing. What do you suppose happened to it?"

Rick climbed out of his bed and padded across the floor to his cupboard and opened the door, reached inside and brought out the notebook. Jas' notebook.

"What the hell are you doing with that?" I asked Rick, trying not to raise my voice.

"It's a long story," he grinned.

"That's a damn stupid and illegal thing you've done Rick," I said, reaching over to get it from him. "When did you steal that, and why didn't you hand it over to the police when they searched his room?"

"I found a key that fitted his bedside cabinet, ages ago and took the notebook, right after Howard's party. I hid it so that Jas couldn't take it with him. When the police came, I couldn't exactly just say - oh here, I stole this, but you can have it now. It's a really insightful read."

"Come on, Rick," I prodded. "What are we going to do? We have to find a way and give it to them."

"Well,"he groaned, knowing that no explanation would seem sensible.

"You have to read it first... all of it, right down to the last page. It explains everything he felt and did. You feature quite a lot. He was very jealous of you. Hated us, but loved you, and more than just brotherly love, mate."

"You know, Rick," I pronounced, grimacing happily as he flicked through the pages, "you do some really dumb shit, even for a Canadian."

"We'll have to say that we have only just found it, behind the sofa or something," I continued, trying to sound convincing. "We can say that Jas obviously wanted to hide it, but not in his own room."

"What? Is that it then?"

"I think some of the others should read it first too," he said slowly, looking at me determinedly. "I think Carmen should. She was going to be next, and Liz certainly should. He failed to kill me and Howard, more through bad luck but he had to kill Lisa, she was carrying his child. George was easy. Liz though! I don't understand his hatred for her. She liked Jas, she didn't have anything to do with you …. did she, Peter?"

"No, not at all. That's what doesn't make any sense. Carmen I could understand, but why Liz?"

Rick opened the notebook and ran through the pages up to the penultimate one.

"Here read this." He said, handing the book to me.

Darling Peter,

If you ever get to read this, it is to tell you my dear friend (or as your Carmen would say - mon cher ami), that I have discovered that I have been betrayed by another person, another 'friend' of yours.

I know that Liz wants you as much as Carmen does.

Up to this time, I have not learned the reason for why she does, but even without some understanding of her motive for doing those terrible things to me, I know this is true. Lisa told me before I killed her.

She will be sorry, and so will you!

I felt cold and my hands were trembling a little as I handed the book back to him.

Why? Even as I formed the question in my mind, I knew the answer. I suddenly remembered a face staring at her with inexplicable hatred. It was the face of Jas. I remembered that I had seen him watching her, on the day we met in the yacht club. I remember the malignant hate that had filled his eyes as he watched me with her, and watched me laugh with her. She introduced me to Carmen.. That's what I wanted her to do. He must have thought it was all her doing, her fault. I wondered whether she had rejected him as well, before he became close to Lisa.

"We'll let Liz and Carmen read this tomorrow, and then YOU will take it to the police station."

I closed my mind around the thought as a man might close his hand around the hilt of a knife. I cried the joys and agonies of those who had died and those that had not. Suddenly, Carmen was beside me, woken by our talking and my heart soared in response. Rick looked up from the book to meet my eyes, and nodded slowly. I smiled and turned to look into Carmen's beautiful face. And God help me, I was content and unafraid and almost happy.

Chapter 22

Rick had decided that it was time for him to leave. His cousin had offered to provide him with some work on his farm for the rest of the summer, and under the circumstances, he had agreed to take up the offer, before deciding what to do, and where to go next.

He had played a huge part in my life over the past few months, and I was very grateful. His soft voice had been ceaseless, well mainly, unless he had been shouting at Jas, often explaining what he saw, and all that he knew.

He told me that more people would have died, if it hadn't been for me. He was adamant that we all had destinies planned out for us. Some would be good and some perhaps not so.

We had been the survivors, even though we had all been scarred. But we were alive, Rick said, us few. We were the lucky ones, the ones that 'hate' hadn't reached. There is a truth that is deeper than experience.

It's beyond what we see, or even what we feel. It's an order of truth that separates reality from perception.

We are helpless in the face of it; and the cost of knowing it, like the cost of knowing love, is sometimes greater than any heart would willingly pay.

It doesn't always help us to love the world, but it does prevent us from hating it. Jas didn't manage to keep his love from turning into hate. He couldn't share his truth, his love, that was in his heart.

He couldn't prevent it from turning into hate.

The evening before I was due to go back to Sussex, Carmen came to see me.

She stood at the front door.

Under the streetlamp her hazel eyes were jewels of love and desire. Her lips widened in the half smile that I knew so well and again my heart began to hope.

"Tomorrow," she said, "When you go back to your life in Sussex, try to relax completely, and go with the experience. Just... let yourself so. Sometimes, you have to surrender before you win.

"You've always got some wise advice, haven't you?" I said, laughing gently as I stroked her cheek.

"That's not wise, Peter. I think wisdom is very overrated. I've told you this before. I may be just a little cleverer than most." She said, laughing at me now.

"Okay, I'm going. Come and see me in Edinburgh sometime. I will look forward to it. I really will."

She kissed me on my cheek, and turned away. I couldn't obey the impulse to hold her in my arms one last time and kiss her lips. I watched her walk, her dark silhouette a part of the night itself.

She moved under the next street light and it was as if my watching eyes had made her shadow come to life, as if my heart alone had painted her from darkness with the light and colours of love.

She turned once to see that I was watching her, before she softly climbed into her car and shut the door.

The last hour with her was my truth test. I asked myself if I'd passed it, or if I'd failed. I still think about it all these years later.

I closed the door to the cottage and in my room, I lay down to sleep.

The move back down south was a hard solution, but a practical one.

I felt relieved and optimistic about it, and I was very tired. I should've slept well, but my dreams that night were violent and troubled.

Carmen had told me once, that a dream is the place where a wish and a fear meet.

When the wish and the fear are exactly the same, she said, *we call the dream a nightmare.*

About the Author

DAVID I BROWN was born in 1953 and was educated in Harrogate, Yorkshire and then London. He spent his early career working for large global manufacturing businesses, which took him to many places around the world. Later, he started his own consultancy in risk management, continuing to travel widely.

His business and travel helped him keep focused when, in middle age, he discovered he had life-threatening cancer, which drove him to write his first-ever book, a memoir. He then wrote a short novel, light and amusing. It was a joy writing it, he explained, as it enabled him to express his earlier adventures and embellish his thoughts about some of the characters he had met whilst travelling. Two more followed and this one is his fourth.

He has been married to Grace since 1981, has three grown-up daughters and is now a retired grandfather, with three wonderful and adorable grandchildren. He and his wife live in Buckinghamshire, England, spending time at their seaside retreat on the West Sussex coast and travelling across the world whenever possible.

The Cover Image.

229

The cover of this book was painted in water colours by the author. It was taken from a photograph when the author was working up in Berwick in his early twenties.

Printed in Great Britain
by Amazon

17140197R00132